SAMUEL W. TAYLOR

ASPEN BOOKS

Heaven Knows Why
©1994 by Samuel W. Taylor
All rights reserved
Printed in the United States of America

No portion of this book may be reproduced in any form
without written permission from the publisher,
Aspen Books, 6211 South 380 West,
Murray, UT 84107

Library of Congress Cataloging-in-Publication Data

Taylor, Samuel Woolley, 1907–
Heaven knows why! / by Samuel W. Taylor

    p.   cm.
ISBN 1-56236-217-8
I. Title.
PS3570.A954H4 1994
813'.54—dc20

                94-38202
                CIP

Cover design by Brian Bean
Cover illustration by Jim Madsen

INTRODUCTION TO THE SECOND EDITION

Back in 1948, the readers of *Collier's* magazine were offered something brand new in popular literature. It was a six-part serial, *The Mysterious Way*, set in a rural Mormon community. That it was fiction made it unusual, because very few Mormon novels had been written. Also, it was about modern life, not about the pioneers. More, the story sprang from situations and characters relating to the Latter-day Saint culture.

But what made it unique was that it was funny. Up until that time, the Saints were accustomed to two types of literature: "for" or "against," black or white, favorable or unfavorable, pro-Mormon or anti-Mormon. In either case, deadly serious. Humor was unknown.

My story was therefore somewhat of a shock. Wasn't it, some felt, Making Light of Sacred Things?

Well, no. I could see no reason why I shouldn't write about my people, with their foibles and conceits, in the same manner that Jewish, Catholic and Protestant authors did theirs. (And do you recall that even Joseph Smith admitted to "foibles"?) I didn't believe that everything written about the people I knew should be either a hard-sell missionary tract or a publicity handout (neither of which could be published for the general reading public of the "outside world").

It was no coincidence that a large percentage of Broadway plays were about Jews. This is because New York has a large Jewish population which supports the theater. With motion pictures, *Going My Way* was a memorable film about Catholic priests. *The Sound of Music* was about a girl who left a convent because of love. *Fiddler on the Roof* was about cultural problems of Jews in Russia. *Friendly Persuasion* was about the Quakers.

This list could be a long one—for other cultures, but not for the Mormons. There had been no Mormon play on Broadway, no Mormon motion picture except *Brigham Young*; and, with the notable exceptions of Vardis Fisher's *Children of God* and Maurine Whipple's *The Giant Joshua*, I cannot recall any fiction written by Mormons for the world at large. These both were historical. There was nothing published about the modern culture.

Thus, *The Mysterious Way* ploughed new literary soil. If it turned up Mormons who weren't the customary cardboard stereotypes of people between the covers of the books in your ward display case—well, I was portraying my people as I knew them, not as we might wish them to be.

Matter of fact, all the characters in my novel were based upon representative types of people I knew personally. This doesn't mean I used people as they actually were. Every individual is entirely too complex and contradictory for fiction. I learned this while writing another book, in which I took a leading character straight from life. The editor was enthusiastic about the story. "But," he said, "you'll have to do something about Buster. I simply can't believe him." So for credibility I had to simplify and fictionalize the only true character.

When *The Mysterious Way* was running in *Collier's*, the great indoor sport throughout Mormon country was figuring out the *actual* locale and the *true* identities of the fictional characters. Many readers were convinced that I had merely changed the names of living people, some of them prominent. In fact, there seemed to be some confusion regarding fiction, as such. One reader demanded to know the true name and address of a character portrayed as an apostate, perhaps with the idea of putting the missionaries on him.

In any event, as readers of the Intermountain West positively identified the *real* locale and *actual* characters at various locations in Utah, Idaho, Nevada, Wyoming, Arizona and New Mexico, it became obvious that my story rang true all over Mormon country. Perhaps this was what made some readers bristle; few of us like our own faces in the mirror.

This was my first novel, and one thing I've learned since then is that Mormons are passionately proud of being the Peculiar People, but heaven help the author who points out the peculiarities. For example, our struggles over the Word of Wisdom, which played a prominent part in my story. We can sit around all night howling about Word of Wisdom stories—but should we put them in print? Well, what else so typifies our culture? We all know the returned missionary who would rather sacrifice his right arm than drink a Coke, but who is very fond of Pepsi. Or the man with eighty pounds of excess fat pounding the pulpit about the Lord's law of health. Or—well, you know a hundred of them.

The basic story of *The Mysterious Way* was implicit in the title: it concerned the power of faith. However, when it came time for book publication, the editor required a different title. For a magazine, the title isn't really important. Any novel serialized in *Collier's* was automatically a bestseller, with several million readers. A book, however, is born naked and alone. Unless it becomes a book club selection, it must depend largely on people who prowl bookstores, pluck a likely volume off the shelf, and buy it after reading the blurb on the dust cover. So a catchy title is vital. Thus, as a book, my novel became *Heaven Knows Why*.

The book was chosen as an alternate selection of the Literary Guild, who touted it as being "in the best tradition of leisurely American humor," and "a funny book that is funny."

Subsequently, in a survey of Mormon literature, Dr. Kenneth Hunsaker of Utah State University called it the "best Mormon novel." While I was of course pleased by this recognition, I was fully aware of the lack of competition. This was brought home recently when Dr. Richard H. Cracroft of Brigham Young University phoned me regarding a paper he was preparing on "Samuel W. Taylor and *Heaven Knows Why*." My book, he explained, still stood alone after thirty-odd years. It was unique. There simply *wasn't* another humorous Mormon novel.

He suggested that in the intervening decades the Mormons have matured to the point where we can now chuckle rather than bristle at some of the foibles and conceits of our culture.

If he's wrong, heaven help me.

Samuel W. Taylor
Redwood City, California

CHAPTER ONE

Everybody is happy in heaven. That's what makes it heaven. The only shadow on the ecstasy of old Moroni Skinner was that he'd died without having a son. His only child had been a girl, and she'd married the valley trash, Jared Whitetop, much to old Moroni's dismay. She should have known better, and anyhow it was a snide trick after her father had passed on and couldn't do much about it. Jared Whitetop was so confounded lazy that for a long time it seemed as if he didn't have the gumption to father a child. But eventually he did. It was a boy child, named Jackson Skinner Whitetop, and old Moroni Skinner's happiness in heaven was complete. Until, that is, the boy grew up.

Jackson grew into a fine healthy lad, six feet and one inch tall. And he had the Skinner mouth. But from there on he took after his daddy. He was trashy. Plain, downright lazy. The way he was headed, he'd never amount to a hill of beans.

Old Moroni Skinner kept close check. He worked in the Compiling Office of the Accounting Section of the Current History Division of the Records Department, and it was a very busy place because every act and thought of everybody on earth had to be put on the books and cross-indexed, and even the fall of a sparrow had to be noted, for some reason Moroni couldn't understand. He felt there was entirely too much paperwork to the whole shebang. But still his job put him in a fine position to keep track of his grandson. Yet the more he looked the less he saw. Young Jackson was turning out wrong.

When the war came along, old Moroni Skinner was both happy and dismayed. He thought the Army would make a man of the boy, but he didn't want Jackson to be killed. He figured it was going to be a busy period, neglecting his work to protect the boy with heavenly signs and premonitions. But, luckily, and without any help, Jackson landed in a safe headquarters overseas and came out of the war with nothing worse than the habit of smoking, a taste for coffee, and a great skill at gin rummy.

Young Jackson's parents had died in a car wreck while the boy was away, and Moroni felt that responsibility would help, also. But Jackson came out of the Army lazier and more shiftless than he'd gone in; an Army headquarters places a premium on men who pass the buckslip, and anyone who tries to work is scorned as an eager beaver. When Jackson got back home he rested up, and the longer he rested up the more he needed rest. The ranch kept right on going to rack and ruin. The ranch old Moroni had worked so hard to build up. So long as Jackson had food in his belly and a roof over his head and a book to read he didn't seem to care. And such books! Trash. While he was away he'd given Henry Brown power of attorney to run his affairs, and after he got back he just let it ride. He lolled about, resting, month after month after month, and he didn't even realize that Henry Brown was stealing the place out from under him.

Moroni's work suffered. He got to moping. The auditors found a couple of small mistakes in his records. The Office Chief had him on the carpet and told him there were plenty of hard-working angels who'd be glad to have his job. His wife Lucy began pecking at him. Did he want to get left behind while all their friends went on to greater glory? When the opening came for Chief Checker of the Compiling Office, another angel was put in the job over his head.

Lucy came out of the house one day while Moroni was sitting with his chin in his hands on the big gold boulder in the backyard. "Moroni, I declare! What's got into you? You haven't touched your harp in weeks, and the concert coming up. Don't you ever want to go on to greater glory? Not to mention the leak in the roof. And when are you going to haul in that load of diamonds for the rock garden?"

"I keep thinking about our grandson," Moroni muttered.

"You worrying about Jackson and his brief span on earth, and we got all eternity to worry about! If you'd attend to your own affairs and let other people tend to theirs, you'd be Chief Checker of the Office right now and I could hold up my head in public. And anyhow, the job rates a bigger house."

"I like this house. It's homey."

"When you went through your earthly trials nobody up here worried none about you!" Lucy declared.

"That's just it, Lucy—somebody did."

"What?" Lucy put her fists on her hips. "Well, Moroni Skinner, I declare! Married on earth forty-odd year and in heaven, heaven knows how long, and you never told me *that* before."

"It's in the records and it's so," Moroni said defiantly. "When I was a young 'un, a-fore I met you, I was just as shiftless and no 'count as young Jackson. Maybe more. And then one day my father appeared to me from beyond, and he straightened me out."

"Your father?" Lucy was impressed. Moroni's father had known Joseph Smith in Nauvoo and had had four wives and three more sealed to him; with that record on earth his progress in heaven had of course been rapid. "Well, what did he tell you?"

"One thing, he told me who you was and said for me to go and marry you. After that, I guess I just couldn't go far wrong," old Moroni said; he was nobody's fool.

"So that's why you was so bold," Lucy said, pleased. "You knowed all the time that I was destined for you."

"So I been thinking," Moroni said. "Maybe if I appeared on earth to young Jackson—"

"Maybe it's just what the boy needs," Lucy admitted. "Give the lad a good talking to. But," she asked dubiously, "is he worthy of a visitation?"

"He's a Skinner, ain't he? Our own grandson. Of course he's worthy."

"Yes, Moroni. You know it and I know it. But what about the higher ups? Maybe they won't see it that way. They won't let you waste time on a soul who's not deserving. You're behind in your work anyhow."

"I already sent an application through channels," Moroni said.

"And not a word to me! Get a reply back yet?"

Moroni nodded. "Approved. Of course the Destiny Department disapproved my request for the records of what'll happen to the boy in the future—but I just put that in because you always get something disapproved in channels. I didn't expect that. But I got my travel orders."

"Well, then what are you moping about?"

"Limited orders!" Moroni said bitterly, pulling the original and seventeen carbon copies from his shroud. "A one-day pass to earth. One measly day! And look here: it says I'm not allowed to represent any higher authority. Powers limited strictly to materializing in and out of human form at will. I got to check back in before midnight—and it's a long trip, too. And application granted on the understanding no future application on the same subject will ever be submitted. I like that! Work my fool head off around here, and the first time I ask any little favor this is what I get. How do you like that for appreciation? Sometimes I think maybe they're better off in perdition. They do things different there. Down there they get a forty-eight hour pass every week to go out and raise Cain. No wonder the world's in such bad shape."

"You're a fine one to be talking like that," Lucy said. "What more do you want? You got your travel orders, didn't you? If materializing once to young Jackson don't straighten him out, what good would twice be? If he's worthy, he'll come through. What are you sitting there on that rock for? Why don't you get going?"

"But what if he's beyond redemption?" Moroni said. "Well, I'll be back by midnight."

CHAPTER TWO

When Moroni reached the old ranch it was early morning, earth time. He didn't materialize immediately, because Bishop Jensen was knocking at Jackson's door. Moroni wanted to see the boy alone. He whisked through the closed doors and found Jackson asleep in the bedroom.

Jackson opened his eyes at the hammering, lifted the clock which was set face down on a backless chair so it would run, looked at the time, squinted at the grimy window, rolled over and pulled the covers over his head.

"Brother Jackson!" the bishop called. "Brother Jackson!"

Jackson snuggled deeper into the covers.

"His horses are here, Dad!" a girl's voice called. "I'll look around!"

At the sound of the girl's voice, Jackson Skinner Whitetop suddenly sat up straight, leaped from bed, jerked on his Levis, tucked the shirt he'd been sleeping in into them, pulled on his boots, raked a comb through his hair, felt ruefully of his whiskers, and ran to the kitchen door.

Yes, the lad certainly was a fine-looking young buck, Moroni decided. The Skinner mouth. Moroni whisked outside to see the girl whose voice had had such startling effect. She was out behind the henhouse, a rather small and pert girl with large gray eyes and a determined chin— considerably like Lucy had been at her age. Just the girl for Jackson; Moroni approved without reservation. Bishop Jensen's daughter Catherine was prettier, Moroni felt, than the records showed, even with the new system of photo transmission.

"Lazy, good-for-nothing trash," the girl observed aloud, looking about. "Letting a nice place like this run down. Somebody ought to get hold of that man and straighten him out."

"Somebody *will*," Moroni said. Of course she couldn't hear.

"Somebody will," the girl said. "Why did I say that? It won't be that Beulah Hess. If he marries that trash he never will be worth a hill of beans. A pity, too," she added, a bit dreamy and a bit vexed.

Moroni chuckled. Just the girl for Jackson.

"You could snap him out of it," he said.

"I could snap him out of it," the girl said. "Oh, for goodness sake, why did I ever say that? Why did I ever think of such a thing? Me marry that lazy trash! And any- how I'm going to marry Henry Brown," She said with a certain determination.

"You don't love Henry," Moroni said.

"I don't love Henry," the girl said. "Good heavens, what's the matter with me? I think Henry's a *very* fine man."

"Katie!" the bishop called.

"Coming!" The girl went into the house.

Moroni was tickled pink at the way when he spoke an earthly soul repeated it. He went inside with her, and was ashamed to have her see the place. Not that it wasn't well made—the only reason it was still standing was that it *was* well made. Moroni had made it with his own hands, felling the logs in the mountains and hauling them, barking them, adzing them, notching them, setting them up and chinking them; and he'd put six inches of good yellow earth on the roof. But that had been a long time ago. Now rags were stuffed in broken window panes, floors were worn and splintered; the canvas he'd tacked on the inside as a lining was stained with the weather, rotted apart in places, and it still had the same coat of green paint he'd put on it.

Jackson and the bishop were on upended boxes in the kitchen. As Katie came in, Jackson offered her a chair without a back. Jackson had three days of beard and his eyes were puffed with sleep. He certainly was not at his best to meet the girl he should marry.

"As I say," the bishop said to Jackson, "we'll leave for Salt Lake in the morning. We want a day there to get ready. Really ought to have two days, but of course Katie and Henry want to be at the dance tonight. Then the following day they'll go through the Temple, and go to Yellowstone for the honeymoon. Sister Jensen and I want to stay in Salt Lake until after Conference, and we'll need somebody on the place until we get back. I don't like to leave Wishful alone with it all. I'm sure you could handle it, Brother Jackson, for that long. Just the chores."

Jackson considered. "I'd like to help you out, Bishop; but I'm pretty busy."

He yawned, regarding Katie fondly, which is no way to make a girl appreciate a fond look.

"Yes, you're awfully busy," Katie snapped. "Doing what?"

"I realize you've plenty to do, Brother Jackson," the bishop said diplomatically, with a glance of disapproval at his daughter. "But I thought you might give us a hand anyhow, Brother Jackson. Call it a wedding present to Katie and Henry. I'm sure they'd appreciate it. And you owe something to Henry. He took care of your place here and your sheep while you were to war."

"Henry Brown isn't worth Katie's little finger, the crook!" old Moroni snapped indignantly.

"Henry ain't worth rolling in the mud Katie walks through," Jackson said, echoing the unheard message in his own idiom. "The crook!"

"Well, I never," Katie declared.

"What did you say, Brother Jackson?" the bishop asked.

"You're a fine one to talk," Katie pointed out.

Jackson blinked, amazed at himself. "I guess it just slipped out, Bishop." He glanced behind in the manner of a man with the vague suspicion somebody is twisting his arm.

"Naturally I don't think any man is worthy of my Katie," the bishop admitted.

"Now Dad," Katie said.

"But I'd like to know a better man in the valley than Henry Brown."

"Well, I personally am very fond of Henry myself," Jackson admitted. "I didn't mean nothing. Don't know why I said that."

"You called him a crook," the bishop reminded. Bishop Waldo Jensen was a pudgy man with prominent eyes hung with purple bags. He was largely devoid of a sense of humor, and prided himself on a literal mind. "What prompted you to say that, Brother?"

"I guess that was just a joke," Jackson said. "You see a man getting something he really don't deserve you laughingly call him a crook because it's almost a crime to be so lucky."

"Oh, I see; very good." The bishop laughed heartily for three seconds to show he got it. "Well, then, we'll see you in a little while. As soon as you've had breakfast. I appreciate it a great deal. Just the chores." The bishop arose. "Come on, Katie."

Jackson was confused. He hadn't accepted the bishop's proposition and he hadn't intended to say what he had about Henry Brown.

"Just a minute!" old Moroni cried.

"Er—just a minute," Jackson said.

The bishop turned at the door.

"How about taking her to the dance tonight?" Moroni suggested.

"How about picking you up for the dance, Katie?" Jackson said.

"What?" the bishop said. "What was that?"

"Well, I never," Katie said.

Jackson gulped, utterly surprised at himself.

The bishop forced a laugh. "Very funny, Brother Jackson. You're sharp this morning."

"He means it," Moroni said.

"I mean it," Jackson said.

"Well, Brother Jackson."

Katie tossed her head. "Let's go, Dad. I think we've wasted enough time here." They left a miserable and surprised Jackson Whitetop.

As Katie drove south along the valley, old Moroni was in the back seat. The bishop's pouched eyes were puzzled, and he kept glancing at his daughter in a calculating way. "Katie, have you given that fellow any reason for acting the way he did?"

"Dad! That's a fine question to ask me."

"A man certainly doesn't talk like that without reason."

"You know how much I've seen of him. We went out together when he was home on furlough, and a few times after he got back. We all hoped he'd changed. And he's so—well, he's attractive and charming. But he went right back horizontal, and Henry began calling around. It's been a long time."

"Well, he certainly was familiar," the bishop said.

"You're not implying he has cause to be?"

"Well, it certainly surprised *me*."

"It surprised me just as much. I haven't even seen him for ages, except maybe to say hello at the store when I'm in for the mail, and he generally asks for a couple of dances at the monthly shindig. He's a good dancer. He's been going with Beulah Hess for ages."

"He's never been impudent before. Lazy trash from a trashy family, but he's had good manners. In fact that's about the first spunk he's showed in his born life. Trash like that—"

"Who you calling trash?" Moroni demanded. "He's my grandson!"

"Trash?" Katie said. "He's Moroni Skinner's grandson."

"Yes, and Jed Whitetop was his father," the bishop pointed out. "Worthless a man as ever I seen. Young Jackson favors his grandfather some, around the mouth and eyes; but he's his father's boy. Why are you defending him?"

"Why discuss him, anyhow?" Katie said. "After all, Dad, I'm marrying Henry Brown."

"Ha!" said old Moroni, and he whisked away.

"Well, I don't see—" Milo's voice trailed off as he realized he was speaking to the empty desert air. The old man blinked, rubbed his eyes, and squinted. "Well, I'll be doggoned!" He got up and walked the length of the porch, peering along the side of the store. Then he walked around the store, went inside, looked behind the counters on both sides, came out, sat down, and scratched his white thatch. "Either I gone crazy or my eyes are going bad, or that there's the funniest thing ever did happen to me in my born life." His cigar had gone out and he lighted it. Puffing furiously as usual, he mulled the thing over. Yep, sure was a funny thing to happen to a man.

Milo prided himself that he didn't believe in anything or anybody. He had the bitter satisfaction of having discovered that everything and everybody in the world was part of a gigantic fraud. No man was honest. Every hand was against him. With one exception. Gazing south from the store porch, he could see a small square of white picket fence on a little rise in the center of a ten-acre square of meadow land. That meadow was all the property he had left in the world, and the rise in its center was the place where, for fifty-odd years, he and his wife had planned to build a house. They'd spent many a long evening through the years drawing sketches, discussing rooms and closets and alcoves. Milo had never been a good businessman. He'd inherited the ranch and store. It had always been next year, or the year after, when they'd start the house. And with each postponement the plans grew. The farther away it was in actuality, the more golden became the dream. Nothing would be skimped on that house. It would be

built to last. It would be the finest structure in the valley.
And after Abbie had died and a combination of doctor
bills and a lifetime of poor ways took Milo's ranch and
store away and left him merely in the position of a clerk,
he'd managed to hang onto that square of pasture land.
He'd buried Abbie on the house site and put a white picket
fence around her grave.

Milo shrugged uncomfortably. Abbie unhappy over
there? Why should she be? Anyhow, what could *he* do
about it? Why hadn't Moroni left him alone, anyhow? He
didn't want any visitation. Didn't believe in such trash.

CHAPTER FOUR

Moroni traveled about the valley in spirit form. Good to see it all again. Hadn't changed much, except for where the flood had come out of East Canyon years ago. There were still occasional ragged ends of charred lumber protruding from the jumble of rocks left by the flood, an occasional sack of hardened cement with the bag rotted and bleached. The flood had destroyed the materials for the valley church and, old Moroni had always felt, had served everybody danged well right. "The Trouble," as it was always called, was a bunch of foolishness anyhow. If folks couldn't even get together on building a church, they were in pretty sorry shape, and so far as he was concerned, they could fry.

Moroni knew a lot about Henry Brown from the records, and he wanted a look at the man who was scheduled to marry Katie Jensen. He found Henry up East Canyon bumping along the side of a hill in an Army weapons carrier. A sheepherder, clinging for dear life beside him, kept an eye peeled for a likely spot to jump if the car overturned. Henry Brown, amused at the man's fright, picked a path a bit steeper and more bumpy than was absolutely necessary. As he rounded the hill a sheep wagon was ahead, atop a little knoll beyond a grassy hollow. Henry bore into the hollow, and the herder relaxed a bit, saying, "I still like a horse."

Henry Brown had good teeth, and he showed them all when he threw back his head to laugh. "Takes a day on a horse, and we made it in an hour."

Two men came out of the sheep wagon as the weapons carrier bumped into the knoll. "Well, men," Henry said heartily, "how's everything?"

Whitey Jones, the camp mover, looked at the man beside him. "You tell him, Ned." And to Henry: "Me, I was away. I was in for supplies. And anyhow I got your three other camps to move. I can't be here all the time. Ned's the herder, not me."

"What happened, Ned?" Henry asked.

Ned Holt looked down his nose. He was a slight fellow, colorless and with no single strong point visible, the sort of man Nature apparently tosses together out of skimpy odds and ends to fill the quota at the close of a busy day. "Well, I'll tell you, Henry. I had one of my spells. Flat on my back and couldn't move for three days, and Whitey gone. I reckon the sheep scattered pretty bad. Soon's as I could walk I went out after 'em."

"We lost fifty, sixty head," Whitey Jones said.

"Well, damn you!" the herder who'd come with Henry cried to Ned Holt. "Getting so's I'm afraid to take my week off!" He turned to Henry hotly. "Henry, I'm going to speak my piece and I don't care what nobody thinks about it! I've been fixing to say my say and I'm a-going to do it! This is your herd; you own the sheep. But it's my sheep, too, in a way. I live with 'em. I got no kick a-coming with you as a boss. Neither has your other herders. You treat us fine and we get the best grub money can buy. But how do you think we feel when we take our week off and this drunken bum of a Ned Holt takes over as relief? We're afraid to come back to the herd. Like as not something's happened. Sheep lost. Coyotes into the lambs. Scattered in a storm. I don't know why you put up with it. If you want to give Ned a job, keep him around your place where he can't do no damage. Well, that's my piece," the herder growled truculently. "If you want to give me my time, it's O.K. But it's how I feel and it's how the other boys feel too."

"I'm behind you there, Mack," Whitey Jones said. "Henry, we're trying to do a job for you. But when Ned's on relief I can't always just stick with his camp. And the minute he's alone he's apt to have one of his spells." He jerked his chin significantly at three empty whiskey bottles by the wheel of the wagon.

"I'm sorry, Henry," Ned Holt said.

"Ned, you told me the last time it wouldn't happen again," Henry said, more in sorrow than anger. "Well, I guess it can't be helped now; let's go."

As the vehicle bumped down the hill, the camp mover and the herder met each other's eye and shrugged. "Beats me," the herder said. "I'd get rid of that drunken bum. Would of done it years ago."

"Well," Whitey Jones said, "they say that Ned Holt once done something for Henry. And Henry he sure never forgot."

"A fine man," the herder said. "That's the only thing

wrong with Henry. He's too good for his own good."

Moroni Skinner was perched on the hood of the weapons carrier. "Henry," Ned Holt said, "you see how it is? We can't keep on like this."

"Everything go off O.K.?"

"Well, yes," Ned agreed reluctantly. "I cut 'em out at night and met the trucks at the logging road." He got a sheaf of bills from his pocket and passed them to Henry Brown. Henry counted them and put them in his own pocket. Moroni would have been amazed at a man stealing his own sheep, except that he knew from the records that Henry Brown did it for income-tax purposes. Henry was firm in the belief that the government was run by a bunch of robbers. This belief he held in common with a considerable number of people, and, like some of them, he did something about it. Henry began to whistle.

"Henry," Ned Holt said.

"Yeah?"

Ned Holt swallowed, steeled himself, and blurted: "Henry, what say we call it square?"

Henry glanced at the small man. "Square? Ain't we square?"

"I don't mean it that way, Henry. You been square with me. But a man can push luck too far. I'm getting scared. Times I don't sleep good for thinking about it."

Henry threw back his head to laugh. The laugh was a trifle to loud. Henry himself had wondered at times at his phenomenal luck. Everything had come his way. He'd started with nothing, and now he was the biggest man in the valley, next to the bishop. First counselor in the bishopric; all fixed to marry Katie; three sheep herds of his own and another practically his for the asking; and with—let's see now, counting this deal—with eighty-three thousand dollars cash tucked away which the government knew nothing at all about. Yes, he'd done all right. Henry told himself, emphatically at times, that he was just a little smarter and a little sharper and a harder worker than most men. But still he had the feeling that Lady Luck had ridden on his shoulder. He didn't like to think of that, or to speculate on what would happen if she flew away.

"There's no risk, Ned," he pointed out. "What if somebody caught you delivering to those trucks? I'd back you. There's no law yet that a man can't sell his own sheep."

"I been figuring," Ned Holt said doggedly. "Figure on getting a little place of my own. And you're getting married. A single man don't mind so much, but when he gets married it's different."

"I'll worry about my wife."

"Yeah; but what about mine?"

"Yours?" Henry said. "Well! Who's the lucky girl? Congratulations!"

"Well, I ain't exactly asked her yet. Beulah Hess."

"Beulah Hess?" Henry said; then he added the proper thing: "A fine girl."

"But I know she won't have me unless I straighten out. And Jackson Whitetop's apt to up and get her in the meanwhile."

Henry laughed. "That lazy trash?"

"At least he's honest," Moroni snapped.

"At least he's honest," Ned Holt said.

"Honest? What's eating you? What's wrong about a man keeping his own money that he's earned fair and square, instead of forking it over to a bunch of robbing politicians who never did an honest day's work in their lives?"

"I mean—well, Henry, you know how it's like in the valley. A man ain't in good with the Church, hereabouts, he don't get along with the right people. Take me. I never smoked a cigarette in my life, and I can't drink on account of liquor makes me sick. But I got to make out like I do to account for them spells at the sheep camps. So every time there's a dance I got to go out in the shed behind the schoolhouse with the boys and drink a pint flask of tea. And then maybe somebody urges a drink on me and I can't hardly refuse, and I get sick. I got a awful reputation hereabouts, Henry."

"Well, it's paid off, hasn't it?"

"But I know Beulah won't have me until I straighten up. So I got to reform. I can't have no more spells. This was my last one. Why don't we call it square and quit?"

Moroni felt sorry for Ned Holt. Ned was such an inadequate little man. And his cut, for ruining his local reputation with the Saints and doing the dirty work, was a pittance compared to Henry's.

"Sure, Ned," Henry said soothingly. "I guess you're right." No use opposing the man now. Let him get his girl. A married man always finds out two can't live as cheaply as one. Ned would be glad for a little extra change.

Henry drove into the valley from East Canyon and let Ned Holt off at the Hess place. Moroni whisked inside to take a good look at the girl Jackson had been seeing.

Beulah Hess was on the leather sofa in the front room, reading a love magazine. She was a pretty girl, but grimy; definitely grimy. She had an old bathrobe over her nightgown and she hadn't combed her hair. As the car swung into the yard she scurried into her bedroom. "It's Ned Holt," her mother said, peering out a front window.

"Why does he come around this time of day when I'm in a mess?"

"Maybe he wants to ask you to the dance tonight."

"Let him ask."

"At least he's got a job. He's a hard worker, if he'd straighten up. That's more than I can say of some of the young men who hang around, not mentioning no names."

With amazing speed Beulah underwent transformation. She whipped off her bathrobe and nightgown. Moroni turned away, guiltily wondering if Lucy would find the scene in the records. When he looked back, Beulah had pulled on slacks that covered her grimy legs, a sweater that covered her arms, and was powdering over the grime on her face. She painted her lips, concealed the rat nest of her hair with a kerchief and sauntered out daintily to meet Ned Holt.

"Gee, you're pretty today, Beulah," Ned said worshipfully.

"You came at an awful time, Ned. I look a fright."

This certainly, Moroni felt, wasn't going to be the girl his grandson married. Not if he could help it. He hurried to catch up with the weapons carrier. Henry Brown was speeding across the sage flat toward the bishop's place, whistling in anticipation of visiting a bit with Katie. Ahead on the road was a cloud of yellow dust, and Henry's happy countenance assumed a vexed scowl as a Model T emerged into view. He glanced about, as if considering the possibility of leaving the road and bumping across the sage hummocks, but rejected it as undignified. The Model T held the center of the road. As he turned to the right it turned to meet him. The two cars stopped with a scant yard between the radiators.

"Why, hello Henry!" Anita Smith said, as if she had just seen the other vehicle. She was, Moroni knew, the only one of Nephi Smith's six daughters living at home. Nephi Smith was saddened the way his daughters had turned out; two had run away with Gentiles and three times he'd taken his old .30-30 carbine and his Model T and brought back a scared young fellow to marry one of the others. Which left Anita. But Anita had gone to Salt Lake to work in the small arms plant during the war, and she'd returned with a baby. The father was, she'd explained vaguely, a soldier killed overseas. But everybody knew she didn't receive government checks. Anita Smith, with black hair and sparkling brown eyes, was pert and saucy, and didn't seem at all burdened with the weight of her transgression. The young bloods of the valley who'd got the idea she was easy pickings had received rude surprises. Whoever was the father of her child, she was true to him.

"Why do you stop me like this?" Henry said. "I'm in a hurry."

"I just thought you might like to see little Henry. Just take a peek, Henry. He's asleep in the back."

Henry Brown winced. She'd named the child Henry, and said her phantom husband was named Brown. Henry

Brown is a common enough name, but, still . . . He got out and looked sullenly at the sleeping child. "Ugly little brat."

"There's quite a resemblance, don't you think?"

"For heaven's sake, Anita! For the last time, quit that!" Henry never had understood why she'd wanted to come back to the valley and face people. Or why she'd had the baby in the first place. Henry Brown, to put it bluntly, just never had understood Anita Smith. To him, the affair in Salt Lake had been just an affair. The things he'd told her were just the things you say to any girl you're having an affair with. It had been a terrible shock when she wrote him that she was pregnant, and he realized she'd taken it seriously—that she'd been, as he put it, a damned fool. He'd risen to the occasion like a man, and had immediately sent her special delivery two hundred dollars and the name of an abortionist. If she wanted to have the baby, after that, it was her own affair. He'd washed his hands of the whole business.

"Look here, Anita; I don't like this."

"Don't like what, Henry?" She was all innocence.

"I'll have nothing to do with that brat, and if you think—"

"That's what *you* think!" Moroni said testily.

"That," Anita said, "is what *you* think."

"What? Are you threatening me by any chance?"

"I wouldn't call it that, Henry. I'm getting along all right while waiting."

"What are you waiting for?"

"For you to be a man, you rat!" Moroni said.

"For you to be a man, you rat!" Anita said.

"Oh," Henry said. She'd never been so frank before. "If you think I'll marry you, it'll be a long old day. You just try making trouble. Just try it. We've got the example of your sisters. You try to make trouble and I'll fix you. I'll get the courts to take that child away from you. I'll have you declared not fit to bring the brat up."

"Why, Henry, I believe you're afraid. Why fly off the handle?"

"I just want you to understand."

"I'm sorry to upset you, Henry. I just thought you'd want a look at your child before you got married."

"And don't call that brat my child. How do I know it's mine?"

"Well, if you're going to make a scene, good-bye," Anita said. She backed, swung around his car, and went on, blowing him a kiss sweetly.

"If that rat thinks he can marry Katie Jensen or anybody else except me he can think again!" she declared aloud. "He's a heel, but I want him and he's mine."

"Good girl!" Moroni cried.

Moroni figured he'd dallied enough without getting his mission done here on earth. He was afraid the records might show he'd frittered away his time on an important mission. So he whisked again to Jackson Whitetop's house and, upon arriving, he shook his head with vexation.

CHAPTER FIVE

Jackson was relaxing after breakfast, stretched full length on the old oak bed smoking a brown-paper cigarette and idly listening to the mice running about on the green-canvas ceiling overhead. The ceiling gave Jackson a vague feeling of dissatisfaction. His grandfather had painted the canvas a poisonous green on building the house, and as long as Jackson had lived his parents had disliked the color. You would have thought, they'd said, that old Moroni could have got a decent paint while he was about it.

"Jed," his mother once had said, "you know what I been doing? I been thinking."

"What about, Ma?" his father had said.

"I been looking at that green paint for going on—how long's it been? Anyhow, I don't like it and I never did. I been thinking maybe we could paint it another color. Maybe tan or blue or yellow or something."

"Well now, Ma!" his father had said admiringly. "That's a idea!"

So they'd got out the mail-order catalogue and studied over the color chart and argued all winter just what shade they wanted it. That occupied the winter. Another winter it had been a gasoline lighting system with hollow wires. Another winter it had been bathroom fixtures. Nothing more fun, Jackson felt, than looking over a catalogue with somebody during the winter. Nothing ever came of it; didn't cost you anything. Good wholesome amusement. And educational, too, keeping up on new styles and products. Jackson, shifting lazily on the bed, wished he had a wife to look over the catalogue with. Somebody like Katie Jensen, say. What had got into him, anyhow, saying what he did this morning? Of course he was in love with Katie. Anybody would be. He'd been in love with Katie almost as long as he could remember. And during the war it had almost seemed that something might come of it. She'd gone out with him when he was back on furlough, and a few times after he'd come home after the war. But he'd known he wasn't good enough for Katie. Never would be. Still . . .

"Jackson Skinner Whitetop," Moroni said, materializing.

"That's me." Jackson turned his head curiously, blinked, hitched onto one elbow, and glanced behind Moroni to the door. The lock was long since gone, and the door was fastened on the inside by a wire hooked over a nail. Jackson had hooked the door because of the wind; it was still hooked. "Where'd you come from?"

"I came from beyond."

"Beyond what?" Jackson asked. "How'd you get in?"

"Jackson Skinner Whitetop," Moroni said impressively, "don't you know me?"

Jackson swallowed. He'd always felt the old crayon portrait of Grandpa Skinner in the living room was poor art. Nobody could have a gaze quite that stern and a jaw that uncompromising. Not to mention the mouth. But now he realized that the portrait, whatever it was as art, was a good likeness. "Y-yes, sir," he said. "You're Grandpa S-Skinner. How's—tricks up there, Grandpa? How's Grandma Lucy Skinner?"

"Jackson Skinner Whitetop, I have brought you a message from beyond."

"Yes, Grandpa."

"Jackson Skinner Whitetop, you are lazy, good-for-nothing trash."

Jackson had been called the same by practically everybody, one time or another. Being on familiar ground gave him a trace of courage.

"Yes, sir. Is that all, Grandpa?"

"Jackson Skinner Whitetop, it is time you mended your ways. You are the last of the line. It is time you made something of yourself and got yourself a wife and had children to carry on." Moroni was glad to see the boy scared. He'd been a little uncertain about things, after the casual way Milo Ferguson had taken the visitation.

"Yes, sir, Grandpa. I been thinking about it. I've sort of been going around with Beulah Hess."

"Beulah Hess!" Moroni snorted.

"Yes, sir, I know. She's no prize, but who am I?"

"Who are you? Why, you're a Skinner, that's who you are! Nothing's too good for a Skinner! Why, when I started courting Lucy—Anyhow, you don't love Beulah Hess."

"No, sir, I don't. But who else would marry the likes of me, Grandpa? Even Beulah's sort of undecided between me and Ned Holt, and he's only a sheepherder. I don't rate very high, Grandpa. Unless I went off somewheres where I'm not known."

"Look here, Jackson Skinner Whitetop! I settled this ranch and there's no better place in the valley, if it's run right. You stay here and build it up, and marry a nice valley girl. Fix the house up for her, get things in shape. And hop to it! Don't lay there like a lazy bump on a log!"

"Right now, Grandpa?"

"Right now!"

Jackson got up. He was surprised to find his eyes level with the determined gaze of Grandpa Skinner. Of course Jackson was six feet and one inch tall, but he'd always thought of the fabled Grandpa Skinner as towering above him.

"What I did, you can do," Moroni said. "I was trash before I married my Lucy and she made something out of me. You can do the same."

"Who, Grandpa?"

"Lucy—your Grandmother Skinner."

"I mean, who would I marry? No really first rate girl in the valley would have me."

"Jackson, I'm here to get such notions out of your thick head? You're my grandson. Now, what girl would you want?"

"Well—" Jackson said, studying his bare toes.

"Never mind, I know. And I heartily approve."

"You mean. . ." Jackson couldn't utter it.

"Of course I mean the bishop's daughter, Catherine. There's the girl for you, Jackson."

"Katie Jensen," Jackson breathed. He regarded old Moroni's stern face with some perplexity. Certainly the old fellow didn't seem feeble and unquestionably he'd come from beyond with the message, but still—Katie Jensen! "Grandpa, I'm afraid that's impossible."

"Nothing's impossible, Jackson, for a Skinner!"

"For one thing, the bishop owns a good share of the valley that's worth owning."

"Of course; that's why he's bishop," Moroni said. "Couldn't marry into a finer family. Good solid folks, the Jensens."

"Oh, yes, sir; but the bishop's a hard working man. He's got no use for lazy trash like me, Grandpa."

Jackson, that's what I'm telling you. You're *not* lazy trash. Not any more. From now on, you're a hustler."

"If you say so, Grandpa. But, now—Katie's the prettiest, nicest, swellest girl in the whole valley."

"Certainly." Moroni's stern visage relaxed. "Fine a girl as ever I seen. That's why you'll marry her."

"But for me to marry Katie—"

"Jackson Skinner Whitetop, I don't intend to stand here arguing with you! I'm telling you to straighten up, fix up your place, and marry Katie Jensen. That is my message. Is it clear enough?"

"Yes, Grandpa," Jackson said. "But she's engaged to marry Henry Brown."

"Henry Brown isn't fit to roll in the mud she walks through," Moroni said.

"Eh?" Jackson said, guessing what had prompted him to say what he had earlier in the morning. "But, Grandpa, it's all arranged. They're going to Salt Lake in the morning. And next day they're going through the Temple. It's too late to do anything, now."

"Jackson Skinner Whitetop, I have given you a message!"

"Yes, sir. But—how do I do it?"

"That is up to you," Moroni said sternly. He wished he'd got permission from the Destiny Department for at least a peek into the boy's future. Also, Moroni had the uncomfortable feeling that perhaps he was giving the lad a hunk too big to chew. Of course he *should* marry Katie Jensen; any fool could see that. Katie shouldn't marry Henry Brown. But it would take some doing . . . Moroni chided himself for lack of faith. The boy was a Skinner; of course he'd come through! "You will find a way," he said. "That is all, Jackson."

"Grandpa?"

"Well, what is it?"

"Grandpa, now you're here, I wonder can I ask you a question?"

"Go ahead."

"It's something Ma and Pa wondered about, too." Jackson indicated the room with a wave of his hand. "Grandpa, why did you paint it green?"

"Why did I paint it green?" Old Moroni Skinner sputtered. "Is that all you got on your mind to ask a visitor from beyond? I painted it green because I wanted it green! Good-bye!" and he was gone. Why did he paint the house green? Why, that good-for-nothing lazy trash! Maybe, Moroni felt, he'd gone through all the trouble for nothing. Maybe Jackson didn't have it in him. But he'd done the best he could. From now on, it was up to the boy.

Moroni returned to heaven with a clear conscience. He'd done his duty.

CHAPTER SIX

Jackson was not a little awed. Grandpa Skinner was gone; just gone. Here one instant, gone the next. The wire loop of the door was still hooked over the nail. Overhead the mice were scurrying about. A chicken cackled outside. Jackson looked at himself wonderingly in the piece of mirror fastened to the wall. In a way, his face resembled Grandpa Skinner's. It was squarish, with steady eyes and a firm jaw; he hadn't noticed the resemblance before. He wondered if he could live up to the promise of that face. And then he chided himself for the thought. Of course he could; he'd had a visitation, hadn't he? There was nothing to worry about. It would all come true.

"Katie Jensen," he said dreamily. "Mrs. Katie Whitetop. Mrs. Jackson Whitetop—" It was sure good to know there was nothing to worry about. If it was going to happen, then it would. He cast himself happily upon the bed to wait for it.

The bed had seen better days. Much better days. The old oak frame was held together by a bit of bailing wire and a nail here and there, and except for his bemused state Jackson never would have flung himself upon it with such abandoned ecstasy. It uttered a loud screak and collapsed, and Jackson fought clear, rubbing a lump on the back of his head where the oak headboard had hit him.

"Well, all right, Grandpa," he muttered. "I can take a hint."

He shaved and put on his best boots, a fresh pair of Levis, a clean shirt, and his big hat. Then he took off the hat because it hurt the bump on his head. Then he put the hat back on because he thought maybe he needed a reminder, for a little while. He roped his buckboard team in the meadow, hitched up, and drove south along the valley road, whistling happily.

At the store, old Milo Ferguson was sitting on the porch smoking a cigar furiously. "Out early this morning, Jack," Milo said in the manner of one uttering a truth with hidden meanings. "For you."

"Got a considerable to do today." Jackson got out the makings. "Where's Henry?"

"Henry he's gallivanting around getting ready to leave for Salt Lake in the morning. Why?"

"If you see him before I do, tell him I'd like to settle up. Figure on getting married up."

"Don't say?" Milo observed casually, squinting one eye.

"Yep. Figure on getting hitched to Katie Jensen."

To Jackson's surprise, Milo evinced no surprise at all. "Hmm, don't say?" Milo observed. "Nice girl."

"Can't kick," admitted Jackson. His cigarette rolled, he pushed back his hat to lick it, and the lump on his head twinged. He blinked guiltily at the cigarette; been a long time since he'd given a thought to the Word of Wisdom, but the throb of his head was surely a sign. Reluctantly, he poured the tobacco from the paper back into the sack, jerked the string tight, and put the sack in his shirt pocket. Milo's sharp old eyes missed nothing. "Seeing you," Jackson said, and continued down the yellow road.

"Hmm," Milo mused. "So old Moroni told him to marry Katie, huh?" "Where do *I* come in?" He couldn't figure it. Certainly he wouldn't have had that visitation unless it meant something. Heavenly spirits didn't go around appearing to just anybody, especially apostates, for no good reason.

When Jackson pulled in at the Jensen place, Katie and the old hand, Wishful, were crossing the yard toward the stables. Jackson's eyes softened. His little wife! Cute as a button in Levis, riding boots, and a hickory shirt. He waved. "Hi!"

"Hi, yourself," Katie said. Wishful nodded. Jackson hopped over the wheel to follow them.

"Well, Brother Jackson," the bishop's voice said. Jackson looked about for the bishop, and spotted the eyes peering from their dark pouches from beneath the car standing in the yard.

"Looks like you're busy, sir."

"Always busy. Just checking the car over for the trip."

There was the metallic clang of a slipping wrench. "You misbegotten son of perdition!" the bishop cried. "Barked my knuckle. What's on your mind?"

Jackson wondered how badly the bishop had barked his knuckle, and whether it was better to wait until he was in a better mood or take a chance that the pain had humbled him. He took a chance. "Well, sir, I come to explain about what happened this morning."

"I'm sure it was just a slip of the tongue, Brother Jackson."
The bishop sucked at his knuckle. With help the way it was
these days, he couldn't afford to stand on dignity. And he
needed a man around the place while he was in Salt Lake.
Needed another man steady, for that matter. Wishful was
getting old. "Ready to start work?"

"Well, not exactly. Can I have a word with you in private?"

A drop of oil fell in the bishop's eye. He rubbed the eye
with the barked knuckle. "You illegitimate offspring of an
unnatural union!" he cried, and Jackson admired the man's
ability to cuss without using profanity. The bishop rubbed
the eye with his wrist, peering from beneath the car with the
other eye. "Speak up, Brother Jackson! I've not got all day!"

"Well, sir," Jackson said reluctantly; it certainly was the
wrong psychological moment. "I guess what I said this
morning was sort of a premonition. After you'd left, my
grandfather appeared to me."

"Premonition? Fiddlesticks. You're not worthy of it."

"I know; but my grandfather appeared to me."

"Appeared to you? Which one?"

"Grandfather Skinner."

"Old Moroni Skinner? What did he say?"

"He told me to marry Katie."

The bishop's wrist slowly relaxed and dropped from the
oily eye. He looked at Jackson for a long moment, then
began worming from under the car. He got up, slapped the
dust from his overalls, stripped them off, folded them, and
set them on a front fender. "Come into my office."

The bishop's wife was rolling out biscuits in the kitchen.
"Sure a baker today, Jack."

"Going to be," Jackson said.

The bishop was washing up in the sink. Sister Jensen said, "Guess you'll be to the dance tonight, Jack."

"Wouldn't miss it."

"Bring Beulah Hess, I suppose?"

"Don't suppose I will, Sister Jensen."

"Don't let that sheepherder beat your time, Jack."

"I'm not worried about Ned Holt. I'm taking another girl. Thought I'd take Katie."

From the sink came a loud spluttering sound from the bishop. Sister Jensen cut a series of biscuits with the rim of a tin can. "You're pretty sure about it."

"Yes'm."

"Come into my office, Brother Jackson," the bishop said sharply, and led the way, wiping himself on a towel as he went. The office was off the dining room. The bishop sat in the swivel chair at the roll-top desk and indicated a chair for Jackson. The bishop wiped his face and the back of his neck carefully with the towel, studying Jackson steadily. "Look here, Brother Jackson: when did you last pay your tithing?"

"Tithing? I guess you have the record of that, sir."

"I've got the records, but you ain't on them."

"Well, I guess I never have paid none, sir."

"And I haven't seen hide nor hair of you at church since you got back; or before you went, either."

"No, sir."

The bishop surveyed the tobacco tag dangling on the yellow string from Jackson's shirt pocket. "And you don't obey the Word of Wisdom."

"I reckon I've been a little lax," Jackson admitted with admirable understatement.

The bishop scrubbed his hair with the damp towel and began combing. He was feeling master of the situation. This visitation business was a problem to a man in his position. It was the sacred privilege of any worthy Saint to receive a visitation; that was part of the gospel. Trouble was that some abused the privilege. All you had was a person's word for a thing like that. You had to draw a line between the genuine, hysterical, wishful, and mistaken. Not to mention pure fabrications.

"Brother Jackson, I've been bishop out here longer than you've been alive. I've lived out the gospel as best I could and I've tried to be worthy. But I've never had a visitation in my life, or so much as a prompting. And there's been some high Church officials who never had a visitation, neither. Just why do you suppose an angel would appear to *you*?"

"It beats me, Bishop."

The bishop took a small mirror from the drawer, looked at his oil-smeared eye, and rubbed at it with a corner of the towel. "Too many people in this Church go around claiming to have talked with spirits. Mind you, I'm not a skeptic. I believe in visitations. It would be the greatest thing in my life if I had one myself. But I don't think everybody's worthy. I'm not. And we don't need 'em like we used to. Joseph said that himself. Or I guess it was Brigham—yes, it was Brigham. After Joseph passed on, Brigham Young got up and told the people there'd been too many visitations and he figured he could get along a spell on what was stored up ahead."

"But that was a long time ago," Jackson pointed out. "Maybe we're running short again."

"Take Sister Ormand—a good, devout, God-fearing woman, even if she is an awful gossip and you can't believe a thing she says and a terrible pest in fast meeting—I'm speaking confidentially, you understand. Hear her tell it, God Almighty don't have nothing more to do, nothing else on his mind, than to supply her with messengers from heaven to tell her she'd better wear her rubbers because it's going to rain, or to show her where she put down her glasses, or to give her a new block design for a quilt. Just last Fast Sunday she got up and told how the Lord had prompted her to straighten up the front room, and how it wasn't five minutes later that the ward teachers arrived, and how embarrassed she'd been if they'd come with her front room in a mess.

"I wish everybody had Sister Ormand's faith," the bishop said, regarding Jackson pointedly. "But I feel that she's— well, you might say she's prone to exaggerate common sense and a hunch into something bigger. Me, I figure the good Lord's got something else in His mind, what with the world in the shape it's in, than to bother with Sister Ormand's front room." The bishop put the towel on the desk and the mirror in the drawer. "Brother Jackson, I'm going to speak frank. You're a great disappointment to all of us. I knew your Grandfather Skinner well, and he was a fine man. Strong in the gospel and a hard worker. A real man. Pioneered the valley; brought the first company of Saints in to settle it up. But you've taken after your father. Jed Whitetop was a good man, but—well, Brother Jackson—"

"Yes, sir; I know what you mean. Trashy."

"We've been hoping some of your grandfather's blood would show. We thought the war would bring it out. But—well, Brother Jackson, I guess if we took every last man in the valley, I'd say you'd be the least who deserved a visitation. Except maybe an apostate like Milo Ferguson."

"I sure was surprised, myself," Jackson admitted. "You could of knocked me down when he appeared to me. I was scared."

The bishop gnawed reflectively at his lower lip. He hadn't shaken the boy's story at all. "How did you know it was Moroni Skinner?"

"He come in through a closed door, and when he left he just disappeared. Just there one second and gone the next. In front of my eyes. He told me who he was. And, well, I *knew*."

"Yes," the bishop admitted. "You'd *know*. A thing like that, you'd know. And what did he say? That is, if you can repeat it."

"Oh, yes. That's why I'm here for. He said it was time I made a man of myself, and that I should marry Katie."

"There are a lot of girls named Katie in the world."

"He made it plain. Your daughter Catherine, he said."

"Marry my Katie! Didn't the old fool realize . . . I'm sorry. Brother Jackson. It's not for me to question a thing like that. If he gave you that message, will—that's that. If he did. You realize my position. If he *did* come to you with that message . . . Look here, Jackson Whitetop! Katie's only child and you're nothing but . . ." The bishop paused, his face clearing. In fact, he actually beamed. He put his stubby legs onto the roll-top desk and leaned back in his swivel chair with hands clasped over his paunch. "The Lord moves in a mysterious way, Brother Jackson. Yes, indeed. So old Moroni Skinner appeared to you and told you to marry Katie, eh?"

"Yes, sir. And to straighten myself out."

"Exactly. Exactly. Good enough. You know what that means, of course?"

Jackson didn't; and from the bishop's suddenly complacent attitude he was afraid to learn.

"It means, Brother Jackson, that first you've got to prove yourself worthy of her. Yes, indeed. The Lord wouldn't throw a girl like Katie away on trash. And inasmuch as Katie's going to Salt Lake in the morning and she'll go through the Temple with Henry next day, it don't look like you got too much time. In fact it don't look like you got any time at all, Brother Jackson."

Jackson cracked his knuckles bleakly. "All I know is what he said, sir. He said I'd find a way."

"I'm sure of it," the bishop said. "But I think you've made a natural mistake. A human error. You see, there's often more than one way to take these messages from beyond. Your grandfather told you to marry my Katie. Well, who knows what the years may bring? You're both young, yet. Twenty, thirty, forty years, who can tell?" His attitude clearly showed that whatever the years might bring, he personally would begin to worry about it when the time came.

"No, sir, that's not the way he meant it," Jackson said. "Grandpa said *I* was to marry Katie. He said Henry Brown wasn't worth rolling in the mud she walked through."

"Eh? You said that very thing this morning. Did you know then?"

"No, sir. I guess he was there though, prompting me. Otherwise I'd never of said that. Or asked Katie for a date. You know I ain't been fresh before, Bishop. It just popped out of me, and I didn't know why until Grandpa appeared."

The bishop's feet thumped from the desk to the floor. "See here, Jackson Whitetop! Everything's arranged. And my daughter certainly isn't a flitter-brain to leap from one man to another on the eve of her marriage. Do you suppose you're as good a man as Henry Brown?"

"Well, I'm not as well fixed."

"And you're not as hard a worker. Henry's my first counselor in the bishopric. I've been thinking of retiring, and he's in line. I'm getting along, and I figured it would be sort of a wedding present, Katie starting out as the bishop's wife. What can you offer her?"

"Nothing, sir."

The bishop put his feet onto the desk again. "What am I getting steamed up over, anyhow? Katie wouldn't have you."

"Grandpa Skinner said she would."

"I don't give a hoot! Er—I mean, Brother Jackson, that girl has a mind of her own. Very much so. She wouldn't have you in the first place."

"That's what I wanted to see you about, sir. Then I guess it's all right if I ask her."

"I couldn't stop you if you wanted to make a fool out of yourself. But see here." The bishop squinted his left eye until it almost disappeared in the purple ring. "Brother

Jackson, I've raised my girl according to the gospel. She's sincere and dutiful, even though modern and spirited. What you want to do about this thing is your own business. You've asked my permission to court her. I'm giving it to you on one condition. I don't want you to take advantage of her."

"In what way, sir?"

"Don't tell her anything about this visitation. I don't want her to think it's her duty. If the thing is ordained, it will come to pass without you telling her about it."

"Oh, I wasn't going to say anything, sir. I wasn't going to tell anybody except you."

"See that you don't. This isn't a thing for gossip. And now, how are you going to start on the first part of this message, to straighten up and prove yourself?"

Jackson considered. "I guess I'd ought to pay some tithing. Except I'm broke. But I'll see Henry Brown and find out how much I got coming on my sheep."

"Probably little enough. Poor Henry's had some tough luck with his own herds. And what can you expect, letting somebody else handle your affairs?"

"Henry's a good businessman. He took over during the war and I just never got around to taking things back."

"Too busy, I suppose. Of course any man courting my daughter has to be active in the Church. What are you in the priesthood, Brother Jackson?"

"I guess I'm a deacon."

"You're supposed to be that at the age of twelve. What are you now?"

"Twenty-four."

"Looks like you got twelve years to make up in a hurry. You have to be an elder before you can get married in the Temple. Of course Katie will get married in the Temple. And," the bishop pointed out, "your bishop has got to give you a recommend before you can go through the Temple." The bishop gazed reflectively at the ceiling. The more he discussed the situation the more he felt master of it. "And a man worthy of my daughter would have a decent house to take her to."

"Oh, certainly," Jackson agreed bleakly.

"Not an old tumble-down shack, but a nice house. Plumbing and all. Pioneer days are over."

"Yes, sir."

"Well, that about sizes it up, Brother Jackson. Looks like you've got a job cut out for you. We'll see how things work out. Yes, we'll see how things work out."

"Take some working," Jackson admitted. It had seemed all so simple, before he talked things over with the bishop.

CHAPTER
SEVEN

When Jackson returned to the kitchen, Sister Jensen had a pan of hot biscuits on the table, and was opening a bottle of raspberry jam. "How about a biscuit, Jack?"

"Could sure use it."

She buttered a steaming biscuit and smeared it with jam. Beryl Jensen was a woman with a woman's natural curiosity and a woman's way of getting around her husband. The bishop had the old-fashioned belief in a wife's place. A wife was not to be worried about the details of daily business; in other words, she wouldn't know anything about it. He didn't realize, however, that the little jam closet opening off the back of the pantry had only a thin partition of wallboard between it and his office. Or if he did realize it he thought nothing about it, for it never would occur to him to eavesdrop, and his knowledge of women was very limited indeed. So through the years the bishop had developed a rather awed pride at what he called his wife's intuition. He was constantly amazed at how much she knew of his affairs, and suspected she was of finer stuff than he, and attuned to unseen forces of which he was oblivious. It was a source of sorrow to the bishop that a man in his position should never once in his life have had a premonition or a prompting; on occasion he had followed a hunch, hoping it was a prompting, but invariably his hunches were wrong. Sometimes he wondered if he was worthy.

"Here you go, Jack."

A gentle pressure of the fingers caused the jam to ooze out the sides of the biscuit, so Jackson popped the whole thing into his mouth. "Umm," he mumbled appreciatively.

Sister Jensen watched him closely. A bit of jam oozed from a corner of his mouth and his tongue neatly salvaged it. He was, she realized, the sort of fellow to turn a romantic girl's head, tall, good-looking, and charming. And this cock-and-bull story about a visitation! Beryl Jensen had lived the gospel, and she felt it was a way of life that made people better. But she'd never put too much stock in it as the word of God. That business of Joseph Smith and the golden plates had always been just a bit too much to swallow. It seemed to her that Joseph had made entirely too many mistakes to have been guided by the Lord.

Beryl was seventeen years old and a barmaid at her father's public house, the Lamb and Lion in Burton-upon-Trent, when Mormon missionaries came to town. She had stopped at a street meeting, and from that moment her life had changed. It wasn't what the earnest young fellow with the dark-ringed eyes was saying; it was the way he talked, the way he carried his head; it was everything about him, and she knew the important thing in her life was to see more of him.

That took doing. He couldn't go out with girls while on the mission. He wouldn't have gone out with a barmaid or the daughter of a public-house keeper in any event. The only way she could see more of him was to have him invited to the house. The only way to have him invited was to interest her parents in Mormonism. And that took some doing.

But it all worked out, for Beryl was a determined girl. Her father sold the public-house and came to America as a convert. He settled on a farm near Manti, and never did very well. He didn't know anything but keeping a public-house, and of course he couldn't do that. He didn't know anything about farming the desert either, but farming is something many people think takes no skill. When Waldo Jensen returned from his mission he looked the family up (they had been his only converts), and after a year he married Beryl.

She had felt at times through the years a bit guilty. Not because she had worsened her father's station in life; he, after all, had been firm in the faith and happy about the change. She felt guilty because she had done it all for love, because she wanted a man, and not because of the gospel. She'd tried hard enough. She'd lived the gospel to the letter. She took her share of the load as the bishop's wife. She was head of the Relief Society in the valley. She always directed and played a part in Mutual plays. She defended the gospel. But she didn't really have the faith.

It was this visitation business that she stuck at. Ghosts, is what she called it. That men high in the Church talked with ghosts, were prompted by the Spirit of the Lord— that the very foundation of the Church was based on a ghost story—it was a bit too much. A bit thick. Sticky. Year after year as she heard the good Saints get up in fast meeting to bear their testimonies, telling of such things, she felt secretly that the gospel was a good way of life but it was marred by this ghost business. Sister Ormand, for instance, with the good Lord running little errands for her. And now this worthless Jackson Whitetop had come with his cock-and-bull story about his grandfather's ghost telling him to marry Katie! Well, it was a bit thick. The lazy, good-for-nothing trash! He wasn't worth a hair of Katie's pretty head. He couldn't roll in the mud she walked through.

"Like it?" she said, and put butter and jam in another biscuit.

Jackson popped it into his mouth. "Umm."

"Katie's out in the corral. Going riding a bit. Tell her not to take the bay."

"Umm mumph." Jackson went out.

Beryl Jensen went into the pantry, closed the door gently and, lighting a match, walked the length of the pantry and carefully opened the door of the jam closet. Through the thin partition separating it from the office she heard her husband's voice praying:

"Oh, Lord, give me light in this dark hour. Show me the way and guide my feet into the right path. Give me faith and give me strength to obey Thy will . . ."

The acoustics of the enclosed place made his voice hollow, and as the match burned her fingers and she dropped it, her eye, in the brief instant of its fall, fastened upon an old milk can which she used for storing things to keep them away from mice. In the darkness her mind's eye still saw the milk can. She felt for it, and lowered her face to its brim. Her heart was beating rapidly, and she wondered if she could do the thing which had flashed upon her as a way to save Katie. It was tampering with everything her husband held sacred. But it was for Katie. Anyhow, it was fighting fire with fire. She could counter one ghost with another.

With her face half buried in the neck of the milk can, she spoke in a slow deep voice. She'd always felt, with the comfortable confidence of one who never had to do it, that if she hadn't married Waldo Jensen she would have been a great actress. Her only contact with the theater was through the Mutual plays and giving an occasional reading; but she'd been told she was very good. Now, as she spoke into the can, she hoped she was half as good as she'd always thought she was. The can helped, as did the small closet and the thin partition. But the cards were really stacked by the fact that the bishop beyond the partition would be the last man in the world to doubt. He had spent a lifetime hoping for a sign.

"My son Waldo," she intoned in the lowest, most ghostly voice she could muster.

Beyond the wall, her husband's voice ceased. Presently, as he waited, she heard his fast and terrified breathing. Beryl had a pang of self-reproach, scaring him like this. Poor dear.

"My son Waldo."

"Y-yes. I am h-here. I hear you."

"My son Waldo, are you prepared for a message? Are you humble? Do you have faith?"

"Y-yes. Y-yes. I am." The bishop could hardly speak. "I have faith."

"My son Waldo, I have a message for you. Young Jackson Whitetop desires to marry your daughter Katie. It was right that you should have required him first to make a man of himself. But one thing you overlooked."

"What is that?"

"Before Jackson Whitetop is worthy, he must prove himself and atone for a wasted life. He must settle the Trouble."

"The T-Trouble?"

"That is his task."

"Y-you mean—the Trouble in the valley? The old Trouble?"

"My son Waldo, that is what I mean."

"But—no mere lad could settle that. I've failed, myself, all these years. And I've worked hard, too. Even Apostle Black couldn't do anything about the Trouble."

"My son Waldo, I have spoken. So be it." Beryl Jensen crept quietly from the jam closet, swung the door gently shut, felt her way through the black pantry, and went into the kitchen. She was shaking. But it was for Katie, she told herself. She'd done it for Katie.

CHAPTER EIGHT

Jackson found Wishful sitting on the top pole of the corral watching Katie cut herself a horse. Jackson climbed onto the fence and gazed fondly at his intended. Four horses circled the corral with nervous cunning, and Katie stood in the center with a loop in her hands, slowly turning, waiting. Straight and slim, confident, with an inherent grace of movement. She was, he knew, the only girl he'd ever wanted.

"Your ma says not to take the bay," he advised.

The horse broke into a run. "You idiot!" Katie said. "Don't you know enough to keep your fool mouth shut? Now he's at the fence. He knows I'm after him."

"I knew it, too. Your ma said not to take the bay."

"I heard you. Is that your job here, running errands?"

"Oh, I'm not taking the job. Got too much to do."

"Why don't you do it and keep your mouth shut for just one minute?"

"As quick as you rope it, I want to talk to you."

Katie put her hands on her hips. "All right, now go ahead and chatter. Get it out of your system. I'll rope the horse later."

"It can wait. Go ahead."

The girl again watched the horses who, horse-wise, kept bunched, crowding the pole fence. The sorrel crowded in front of the bay, which wheeled around and made for a gap between the pinto and the blue roan. The girl's wrist flicked and a small loop snaked out and dropped over the bay's neck. The bay stood still and she walked up to it and patted it on the neck. "O.K., Wishful."

The hand took the rope and led the bay to the stable. Katie climbed straddle of the pole fence beside Jackson. "Mother can never understand it's my neck. Don't mind my temper, but it was a pretty silly thing for you to do. You wanted to see me?"

"Yeah. I want you to marry me."

"Mother always wants me to take a kid horse. What's on your mind?"

"Will you marry me?"

"I thought you wanted to talk to me about something?"

"I want you to marry me."

"Marry you? Jack, that's why folks make you out worse than you are. You're always saying the craziest things with a straight face."

"I'm proposing to you. I want you to marry me. I was never more serious in my born life."

She regarded him steadily. "I do believe you are."

"Will you marry me?"

Katie was embarrassed. "But Jack this is, I mean. . . we've known each other all our lives and all—but you've never even so much as—out of a clear sky like this—"

"Katie, I know it's awful sudden," he admitted truthfully.

"But you see I didn't make up my mind until this morning to marry you."

"Oh. You didn't make up your mind. Of course that explains it."

"It just come to me, you might say."

"You didn't let any grass grow under you feet, once you decided."

"Will you marry me?"

"Jack, this is all so absurd. Seriously, I think it's sweet of you, but—"

"No!" he broke in quickly.

"No what?"

"Don't give me an answer now. Don't say anything you'll have to take back."

"Take back?" A small furrow appeared between her eyebrows. She was, he realized, more lovely than he'd dreamed. She had a delicate line of freckles on each cheekbone showing faint through the tan. "I certainly can answer you once and for all, if you want it short and final."

"I want you to think it over before you tell me yes."

"Oh, you do. And why do you suppose I'll say yes?"

"Oh," Jackson said confidently, "you will."

"I never in my life. I never in my born life. You seem to be in charge, general. How long have I got to think it over?"

"Well, I don't want to rush things. We ought to do a little courting, first. We'll go to the dance tonight, and maybe by the time I bring you home you'll know. That ought to be plenty of time to think it over."

"Certainly. We wouldn't want to rush things, but on the other hand, why dillydally?"

"That's how I feel; I'm glad you think the same."

"Once you've made up your mind, why delay the inevitable?"

"Gee, I'm glad you take it this way, Katie."

"There's just one thing. One small thing," Katie said. She turned her left hand slowly while Henry's diamond sparkled on her finger. "Don't you think you've overlooked a minor point, Jack?"

Jackson grinned tolerantly. "That's one reason I'm giving you a little time. You see, you think you're marrying Henry Brown. But you ain't. You got to get used to the idea of marrying me. It'll take a few hours."

"Jack, are you drunk?"

"Just you wait and see. Be seeing you." He hopped from the fence and crossed to his team, whistling merrily. He unlooped the halter rope and climbed over the wheel to the seat.

"Jack!"

Katie was beside the buckboard, her back stiff. "If this is a joke, I don't think I like it. And I especially don't like it if it's not."

"Want to go for a ride?"

She stamped her foot. "For heaven's sake!"

"You just think it over."

"You really mean this as a serious proposal?"

"Nothing else but, honey."

"Don't call me honey!"

"All right, darling."

"There's no use trying to talk to you."

"You're upset. That's why I'm giving you a while to think

it over. I know how it seems to you. I would of done it different, but there wasn't time. If I'd started in courting you in the usual way, I wouldn't of got no place before you'd gone off to Salt Lake and married up with Henry."

"I don't see just why you had to get this silly idea when a girl's already engaged. It's not ethical. Any man who's a gentleman leaves a girl alone when she's engaged."

"Katie, I can't help it," Jackson said truthfully. "I'll see you later. Think about it."

"I've thought about it. You couldn't keep a wife if you had one."

"Things will change."

"They've sure got to hurry."

Jackson wished he wasn't bound by the promise. If she only knew things had to happen, it would save all the silly argument.

Katie began to laugh. "Well, Jack, it's a relief anyhow. Now I know you're normal. You're the only free boy in the valley who hadn't proposed to me, one time or another. Some even did it by mail. You're a little late, but you did come through. I've been a bit worried about you."

If she thought to deflate him by ridicule, she was disappointed. Jackson wheeled his team, waved, blew a kiss, called "Pick you up for the dance!" and rattled away.

Katie wagged her head. The most ridiculous, silly, preposterous, absurd, cheeky, impudent thing that ever happened in her born life! If only he wasn't such worthless trash—

As the bishop's daughter, Katie Jensen had lived a somewhat restricted life. It wasn't that she ever had wanted to do, particularly, what a bishop's daughter shouldn't. She simply was a bit tired of having her personality and individuality submerged to her position. She didn't like to be shoved around; she'd walk the straight and narrow willingly, but she didn't want to be pushed along it. As the bishop's daughter she was a model for the girls in the valley; she was all things good and proper. And she was, she suspected, heartily resented by many girls who had thrown up to them the fact that Katie Jensen wouldn't do this, or say that. Katie yearned at times to do what she damned well pleased. But life had never been like that.

If only Jackson Whitetop wasn't such worthless trash.

As he drove along the valley road, whistling, Jackson felt he never had properly appreciated the beauty of the country. On the east, beyond the gray sweep of the valley, the Wasatch Range rose steeply, green with conifer on the upper reaches and scrub oak below; summer range. To the west were low hills, table-topped, dusty with sage and spotted with gnarled cedar; winter range. The single creek, marked by a green line of willows, flowed from south to north down the valley center. The valley once had been, old-timers said, covered with bunch grass, but overgrazing had let the sage and greasewood take over. Along the bench of the eastern mountains, where once had been the beaches of Lake Bonneville, were the shacks of the dry farmers who made an annual gamble of a year's toil against the caprices of Nature. Far ahead the creek turned east around the corner of the mountains and petered out in the alkali desert.

A streamer of dust ahead resolved into Henry Brown's weapons carrier. Henry stopped alongside the buckboard.

"Where you been keeping yourself, Jack?"

"Resting."

"Don't go trading with them mail-order houses. I can give you the same stuff and you see what you're getting. Drop in when you need something."

"I'll be in today with a list." Jackson figured it was just as well to get the thing over with. "Going to fix the house up for my wife. I'm marrying Katie."

"Yeah," Henry said. "So I hear."

"I mean Katie Jensen."

"Yeah, Milo told me." Henry chuckled. "You're a card, Jack."

"Damn it, I am! I'm going to marry her!"

"Yeah. Well, see you around, Jack." Henry drove on.

"Well, doggone him!" Jackson growled. It was an insult. Henry didn't even take him seriously.

Henry Brown wasn't going to be any pushover. Henry was a hard-driving go-getter. Some folks called him sharp, but sharpness was a quality Jackson admired, for he had none of it himself. Henry had drifted into the valley as a kid of sixteen and had gone to herding sheep for Jackson's father. For nine solid years Henry had drawn three dollars a month cash wages, no more, and taken the rest in sheep. That gave him his start; he had a small herd of his own, and from then on instead of working for Jackson's father he ran the Whitetop sheep on shares, a thing nobody had done before in the valley. When the depression came he was running three herds in addition to his own, being camp mover for all of them, and by the time things got really tight Henry was the only man in the valley with ready cash. He came out of the depression owning all the sheep except a little dab he still ran for the Whitetops for old time's sake, and when the war came along he picked up Milo Ferguson's ranch and store.

Yes, Henry was a go-getter. He was in his middle forties, which to Jackson seemed very ancient to be marrying a girl like Katie, but it was a good match from Katie's viewpoint. Henry wasn't going to be any pushover to beat out for her.

CHAPTER NINE

Jackson drove into his place as if he'd never seen it before. It was, he had to admit, a mess. What a spot to bring a bride! The outbuildings leaned at crazy angles. Only a couple of pole braces kept the stable from collapsing completely. The dirt roof of the old bunkhouse had caved in and he'd been using the logs of the walls for firewood. The log house itself, once the pride of the valley, definitely was an eyesore. The front door was gone and the hole was covered by an old quilt nailed to the frame. The porch floor was rotted and its roof sagged at a missing post. All that remained of the yard fence were two cedar posts with a gate clinging to one of them by a single hinge.

Inside it was worse.

He began figuring up a list of what he'd need, but it was so nice to dream of Katie that he stretched out on the kitchen floor to mull over the happy years ahead. As his head touched the floor the bump throbbed, and he got up reluctantly. Sure, he was willing to get in and work for Katie, but couldn't a man relax for two minutes any more? Grudgingly, he began working again on the list.

He was checking it over when a voice called, "Jack, are you there?" He went out to see Katie riding in. Riding in alone to see him. That never had happened before.

"Well, honey."

She swung off the bay and confronted him angrily. "I think a joke can be carried too far!"

"So do I. What's wrong?"

"You didn't have to tell Henry about it! He thinks it's a big joke. He's telling everybody!"

"Oh, about you marrying me? I didn't tell Henry; Milo did."

"And who told Milo? I don't think it's a bit funny. The whole valley knows it by now. It makes me so mad! Henry's telling it all over!"

"So you and Henry are busting up a'ready."

"I came over here to straighten you out. That's all. How do you suppose I feel? You proposed to me and I turned you down . . ."

"No, you never. You're thinking it over."

"I'm not thinking anything over. No! Do you understand? No, no, no! Is that plain enough! I tried to make it easy on you. After he's got the gate from a girl, a gentleman doesn't go around bragging about how he's going to marry her. I never was so humiliated."

"I made up a list," he said. "Figure on fixing the place up for you. Maybe you'd like to make some suggestions."

"Oh, for heaven's sake, Jack." Katie flung the kitchen door open and strode inside, looking about with contempt and distaste. "All right, if I've got to be nasty. Look at this place! Linoleum worn out and the floor all splinters. That horrible green canvas. Window panes stuffed with rags. Stove held together with baling wire. Do you think any decent girl would live here?"

"It's well built, fix it up a bit."

She cocked her head. "What's that noise up above?"

"Mice."

"Mice? Why don't you get rid of them?"

"Think I will."

"That's a revolutionary decision."

Well, they been sort of company when a man's alone. But now with you marrying me . . "

"Do we have to go into that? Can't you understand?"

"Look at it one way, the place has got flavor."

"Yes, and a smell."

"Now, take that door." He indicated a large and ragged hole in the kitchen door. "That happened before I was born. Pa was away and Ma was here alone. There was a bad Indian on the prowl. Called him Brokenhead. He'd killed a couple of people and hid out in the hills, and used to come in and molest white women when they were alone. He must of seen Pa leave, and he come to the house and tried to get in. He had a gun and when he shot through the door, Ma give it right back at him with a shotgun. That hole's been there ever since. Gives character to the place. I guess that's the only door in the valley with a history like that."

"And so nice and breezy, too," Katie admitted.

"Stuff a gunny sack in it in the winter. What color do you figure we should ought to paint the walls?"

"I haven't the slightest interest in the color of the walls.

Now, Jack," she said, "I think the whole thing has gone far enough. I want you to do the right thing."

"What?"

"You're sort of a dead-pan humorist. And the thing is ridiculous enough. I want you to turn the whole thing off as a joke. Personally, I'm tired of it."

"It's no joke to me."

"It's impossible."

"I can see how it looks. But it's going to happen."

"Am I using words that are too big? I am going to marry Henry, and if I weren't I certainly . . ."

"Do you love Henry?"

"And if I weren't, I certainly know a lot of men who are better bargains than you."

"Do you love Henry?"

"So if you'll please quit this practical joke . . ."

"Do you love Henry?"

"That's none of your business."

"Ha!"

"Ha yourself. You've certainly been anything but lovable. Will you or won't you?"

"You're prettier than I thought."

"Henry was right. He said I was making a mistake to come here."

"Henry is always right. Do you like monotony?"

"Good-bye, Jack."

"Pick you up for the dance."

"I said good-bye." She strode out angrily, flung the bridle rein over the bay's neck, and swung up the stirrup. The bay was not a horse to be mounted in careless haste, and

Katie landed on the ground with a grunt. The horse trotted for home.

"I'll catch my team and hitch up the buckboard."

Katie got up, slapped angrily at the seat of her pants. "Don't bother. Good-bye."

She was about a mile down the road, trying not to limp in her riding boots, when Jackson rattled alongside in the buckboard. "Well, hello Katie Jensen, the bishop's daughter," he said nasally. "With your fair hair and large eyes that make my heart go pittypat and your pert little nose and the hint of a dimple on your cheek. I wish I could tell you, Katie, what's in my heart."

"That doesn't sound like a radio play."

"I never said it did. Going far?"

"I like to walk."

"Do you mind if I mosey along alongside?"

"It's a free country."

"What do you think of the United Nations?"

"Why don't you go off somewhere and dig a hole?"

"Let's discuss something. I want to take your mind off your feet. How can we dance tonight if your feet hurt? There's something definitely unromantic about a pretty girl thinking about her feet."

"I won't walk far," she said, looking down the road.

"What do I see a mile down the sage-bordered road?" he said nasally. "Leaving Henry Brown's store is a cloud of yellow dust. It must be a car. It is. It's Henry Brown's weapons carrier, coming fast. Now it makes a turn around the corner of the stack-yard fence. It lurches in a chuck hole. It straightens out. Henry is driving furiously. He is angry with every right to be. Henry Brown, engaged to marry you, finds you gallivanting with the valley trash. Here he is now. He slams on his brakes and skids to a stop. His brow is black. Hello, Henry Brown, owner of the valley store and biggest sheepman in the country. You've come to take Katie away? Well, you'll reckon with me, first."

"Huh?" Henry said.

"He's a radio," Katie explained. "Very funny."

"Well, why didn't you give her a ride?" Henry said.

"I'm mean," Jackson said. "She wouldn't meet my price."

"What price?"

"That which is more precious than pearls."

"I caught your horse as it came by," Henry said to Katie. "Get in. I told you not to ride that bay, didn't I?"

"Yes, Henry."

"And I told you not to go down and see Jack in the first place, didn't I?"

"Yes, Henry."

"And it doesn't look right. I told you that."

"Yes, Henry."

"Well, get in."

"Yes, Henry." Katie climbed over the buckboard wheel and sat beside Jackson.

"Aren't you coming with me?" Henry said.

"No, Henry."

"What's the matter?"

"Toodle-oo, Henry."

"I don't get it," Henry said. "Look here, you can't do this!"

"Don't quarrel before the servants, Henry."

"Oh," Henry said. "I'm sorry. It's only because I was

worried about you. On that horse and going down to see this fellow alone."

"I'll be along in a little while, Henry. I haven't ridden in a buckboard since I don't remember when."

"Suit yourself." Henry made a U-turn and sped back.

"Thwarted, Henry Brown roars away," Jackson said nasally. "Having humiliated Katie before an inferior, he is stung by her repulse. Little does Jackson realize in his moment of triumph . . ."

"I believe that's fairly well milked dry," Katie advised.

"Seriously, what do you think of him?"

"Seriously? Why should I tell you?"

"I don't know. Why should you?"

"He's steady and solid. Maybe a bit dull at times, but marriage isn't a matter of sitting around making wisecracks. A little dull and steady solidness is good over the long pull."

"He'll make a good father for your children," Jackson said.

"What's the matter with that? You've got the Hollywood idea. Getting married isn't the end of the story. It's the beginning. The very beginning."

"Being in love is the beginning."

"I've been in love."

"Like that. You've seen a circus."

"I mean, crazily and romantically and not caring about anything but the moment so long as you're with him. He was a soldier and I met him on furlough. There were ten lovely days. He never came back."

"I'm sorry. I didn't know that."

"Nobody does. He never did."

"Maybe if he knew—"

Katie shook her head. "He's dead."

"That's tough."

"And I won't be a fool again," Katie said. "Love is blind, anyhow. It's nothing but glands or something. It has no relationship to a happy marriage. I'm certainly not going to be rushed into a lifetime of regret because of my glands. Henry's a good match and I'm fond of him. We'll get along. He'll be good to me and I understand him. And that's the way to consider marriage. I'm damned if I'm going to be swept off my feet by Mother Nature."

"Say, you're a rebel," Jackson said wonderingly. He'd never thought of her like that.

"I'm a little tired of being shoved around. I'm doing what's best for Katie. Some people think Henry's too old for me. But they all agree it's a good marriage for me. Even you'll have to admit that."

"No argument there." Jackson felt blue. He couldn't possibly offer Katie more in a material way than Henry.

The bay horse was tied to the hitching rack of the store. The people waiting for the mail regarded the arrival of the buckboard with elaborate disinterest. Katie mounted, with care this time, and Jackson went inside. Milo was behind the wicket of the little post office cubbyhole on the left; he was still postmaster, and he helped Henry out in the store.

"Mail ain't sorted yet. You can wait outside with the rest," Milo snapped. Then he leaned across the counter, puffing great clouds of cigar smoke and grinning evilly.

"Doing all right, Jack. Doing all right. Henry won't show it, but he's fit to be tied."

"Got a list here of a few things."

Milo turned to the pigeonholes. "Take care of you when the mail's sorted. You're no better'n nobody else."

Jackson sat on an empty nail keg to wait. He'd never become used to seeing Milo with a cigar. The old man had apostatized while Jackson was away to war. Milo had gone broke from a combination of easy credit, hard luck, and an invalid wife, and he'd thrown religion away along with his faith in humanity in general. Some of the pious Saints said disaster had affected his mind.

Sid Worth drifted in and took an adjoining nail keg. "Well, Romeo," he said to Jackson.

Sid was a dry farmer and the valley funny man. Jackson didn't feel in the mood to follow his lead, and was glad when Milo announced, "Come and get it!" Sid immediately hopped to the wicket for his mail.

Milo handed out the mail. "Well, Jack." He took the list, following down it with his cigar as a pointer, and whistled. "Say, you're really fixing things up proper. Paint, nails, lumber, furniture, harness, linoleum, wall board, gasoline lights, a windmill, pipe, plumbing, refrigerator, tools, stove, separator, disc harrow—what's the water heater for?"

"Bathroom."

"By golly, Jack, you wasn't fooling," Sid Worth said. "Get the place prettied up and all you'll need is a wife." The other men laughed.

"When can I get it?" Jackson asked.

"Give you most of it right now. And the truck goes in to Salt Lake tomorrow." Milo's eyes shifted to the list. "But you got to see Henry."

"What about?"

"I only work here, Jack. He says if you come here for something, you got to see him."

CHAPTER
TEN

Face a bit hot, Jackson crossed the parking area and went through Henry's yard. At the kitchen door he smelled the rich aroma of coffee. Henry obviously was having tough sledding with the Word of Wisdom; he was newer as a Saint than Milo was as an apostate. He'd embraced the gospel when he started going with Katie.

Jackson knocked. "Just a minute," Henry's voice said guiltily.

"Nobody here but us Jacksons, boss."

Henry slipped out the door and closed it behind him. "My back." He put a hand to his back, over the wide belt he always wore on the theory it was good for a trick sacroiliac. "Doctor told me to take a cup of coffee now and then to tone it up."

"Best thing in the world for a back," Jackson said. "The gospel's a wonderful thing. Henry, do you know that Gentile doctors don't realize the value of coffee as a medicine?"

Henry laughed, throwing back his head and showing all his teeth. "That's all right, Jack. What's on your mind?"

Jackson showed his list. "Milo told me to go through channels."

Henry's round face was expressionless. "Quite a list there, Jack. Quite a bill of goods."

"When you get time I figure we'd better settle up my account."

"Take it easy, Jack. That's why I told Milo I wanted to see you. Been wanting to talk things over with you. You know, you haven't even checked up on things since you got back. That's been quite a piece ago. Got a little time?"

"Guess I got a little touchy, Henry. Had the wrong idea, from the way Milo said it."

"Now you're here we might as well look over the books. A man figuring on getting married ought to know where he stands at."

"Never mind the books. What have I got coming?"

"Come in, Jack." They sat at the kitchen table. Henry raised an eyebrow, Jackson nodded, and Henry poured coffee for Jackson and got his own half-filled cup from under the table. "Jack, I just run your sheep because of old times. Your dad he give me my start. Then you went off to war and I figured, well, the least I can do is not charge you anything for running them. I wouldn't take a penny from a man overseas fighting for his country. On the other hand it didn't cost me anything to keep your dab in with my own herds."

"It's good of you, Henry," Jackson said. "But I don't want it like that. I want you to have your regular share for running them."

"No, Jack. Let me do that much for the war effort. Hell knows you did more. And I'm not really giving you anything. I did charge off against your account a percentage of the cost of running the herd, according to the proportion of your sheep to mine. But I never took a penny or a pound of wool for my own time."

"What does it figure to?"

Henry seemed greatly interested in watching his spoon stir his coffee. "Your affairs are in bad shape, Jack. You're into me a little over nine thousand dollars. We'll just call it nine thousand."

"You did all right, Henry. You're a businessman. Of course sheep were good during the war, but you still did all right. I'll just leave it with you and draw on it, if it's O.K.

"Jack," Henry said, watching his spoon, "I said you was into me."

"Into you? Wait a minute."

"Jack, you owe me nine thousand dollars."

"You kidding?"

"It's on the books, Jack. Milo keeps my books. I asked him today how your account stood. I hadn't realized you were in so deep. That's why I wanted to see you."

"Good God, Henry. I had an offer from Young Merrill Littlewall when I was home on furlough, before I went overseas. He offered me fifteen thousand cash for the sheep then. And they've been producing wool and lambs ever since. What's the increase?"

"You haven't got as many sheep as you used to have, Jack. I want you to look at the books. Everything's down in black and white . . ."

"To hell with the books. I can't argue with a set of books. What happened, is what I want to know."

"In the first place, Jack, you wasn't square with the board when you went away. Your folks had always kept into me a little. A little more and a little more. They spent a little more than the sheep earned. Then they died soon after you went away. A sad thing. Both of them at once. That old car wasn't safe; I told them so. Well, there was expense, but I didn't want to talk to you about it at the time. I took care of things. And I figured you'd be gone a while and when you got back I'd have a nice little nest egg built up. You gave me power of attorney. Jack, I did the best I could. I want you to know that. I handled your sheep along with my own."

"You couldn't help but make money on sheep during the war."

Henry smiled sadly. "Jack, you don't know the half of it. Price ceilings. Shortages. We had tough luck three years in a row. And you know what happened this morning? One of my herds lost sixty head and better. Just gone. That's sheep, Jack. Well, one year it was deep snow. We had to haul feed in the winter onto the desert. You know what that means. And we lost a lot of sheep anyhow. That put us behind. Another year it was a blizzard. Ned Holt was herder. And as good a sheepherder as ever was made. Whitey Jones was moving camp, and he came in for supplies and couldn't get back on account of the blizzard. And there was poor Ned Holt out there alone flat on his back sick. One of his spells. We lost a lot of sheep, Jack. The coyotes have been bad. Disease—something hit the sheep and we lost two hundred head before we could bat an eye. One thing after another. And expense, Jack. You don't realize how much it costs to run sheep these days. I didn't know hardly what to do. I used my best judgment. We lost almost half your herd in that one blizzard, aside from the other things. We're both in the same boat, Jack. If it wasn't for the store and my other interests, I don't know where I'd be."

"Why the hell didn't you tell me all this before?" Jackson demanded.

"Why, Jack, you were overseas fighting for our country. I thought I could make it up for you. I've kept account of every penny and I want you to go over the books. Then you got back, and didn't ask me for a settlement, and I figured I could maybe cut it down some at least. But I guess I've no more than broke even for you since you been back. That's the way sheep are, Jack. You can sure lose your shirt."

"You sure lost mine. You done the best you could, but, hell, Henry, this kind of rolls me one."

"Now, about this list of stuff, Jack. If you want food, your credit is always good. I won't stand by and see a man starve to death. But anything else—you see my position, Jack. You're in as far as I can let you go. Your sheep aren't worth more than what you owe me. Not as much. Personally, I'd hate to have to take them in full payment. You see, Jack? I'm getting married. I've got a wife to think about."

"I see, all right. What if I'd brought this list in yesterday morning?"

Henry threw back his head for one of his great laughs. "Jack, you don't think it makes any difference to me? This is strictly business, Jack. I keep business and other thing strictly apart. I'll tell you what, Jack. I'd be losing money but in a way I'm responsible. I feel awful about the whole thing. I'll make you an offer. I'll take title to your sheep and we'll clear off the books. What do you say?"

"I'll think it over."

"I wish you would, Jack. It's a lot of money for me to have out. I'm a little short myself. I can't carry you forever. And I always believe in settling things man to man. Nobody gets anywhere going to court. I don't want to do that. I know you'll see it my way."

"Thanks for the coffee," Jackson said, and went out. Milo was piling goods into the buckboard in front of the store. "Not today," Jackson told him, and began helping unload, feeling foolish under the questioning eyes of the men on the porch. Milo said nothing until the buckboard was bare and Jackson had climbed into the seat; then he observed, "Boy, you've been took," and walked heavily into the store, a bucket of paint in each hand and trailing smoke from the cigar.

CHAPTER ELEVEN

Home, Jackson put up his team and went in the house to make dinner. He fried eggs and bacon, ate them, and was unsatisfied. Coffee was what he wanted. Coffee and a cigarette. And considering the blow he'd just received, he felt that his system needed a pick-up. Yes, sir, Henry's bombshell had bowled him over. Probably in a state of shock. A stimulant was indicated. Definitely.

He put on the coffee pot, and when the aroma came rich and brown he felt better just from the smell. Just what he needed in his condition. He poured a cup, took a delicious sip, set the cup on the edge of the stove, sat down on a box luxuriously and reached in his shirt pocket for tobacco.

"Brother Jackson!"

He jumped, wondering for a guilty moment if Grandpa Skinner had returned.

"I see you are living the Word of Wisdom," the voice said acidly.

The bishop's purple-ringed eyes were peering through the shotgun hole in the kitchen door. The bishop's nose was sniffing the rich brown aroma.

Jackson scratched his chest vigorously instead of pulling out the tobacco. "Just having a cup of Coffee-Near," he said desperately.

"Coffee-Near? What's that?"

"Just an old family recipe. Make it out of wheat and dandelion roots and stuff. Got it from the Indians. Nearest thing to coffee we ever tasted, so we just call it Coffee-Near."

"Don't say." The bishop sniffed at the tantalizing odor wafting through the hole. "Just made out of wholesome grains and roots?"

"And the seed of a berry," Jackson said, not wanting to stretch the truth beyond recognition.

"It smells wonderful," the bishop hinted.

"Well, you have to get used to it," Jackson said disparagingly. "I've drunk it so many years I don't mind it."

The bishop squinted his left eye and smelled in small delicate sniffs, getting the subtle overtones. Then he closed his eyes and drew in a great lungful, his face revealing ecstasy and vast longing. "Jack," he said, in his passion forgetting formality, "have you got an extra drop or two? If that stuff tastes like it smells . . ."

Jackson had no desire to lead the bishop astray. On the other hand it would be no sin on the bishop's part if he didn't know what he was getting. And, surveying the hopeful face at the hole, Jackson decided it would be more cruel to refuse. Too, at the bishop's age a bit of a lift wouldn't hurt him, just once. Jackson also realized that he was not being hospitable.

"Why don't you come in, Bishop, and we'll get another cup."

The bishop was inside with a bound. "Just got a minute," he said, rubbing his hands with anticipation as Jackson poured his cup. "Just grains and berries. Amazing. It smells like the real stuff."

"It don't taste like Army coffee," Jackson said truthfully.

"The war was hard on boys of our faith, Brother Jackson. As I understand it, they generally either had to drink coffee or nothing."

"It was grim. I could hardly bring the stuff to my lips," Jackson said, referring to the infernally hot rim of an aluminum canteen cup. "Cream and sugar?"

"Wait'll I taste it." The bishop took a sip, held it in his mouth with an intent expression, swallowed, and then surrendered. "Ah!" he cried happily, and waved Jackson to a seat. "Nothing, thanks. No camouflage necessary. What a flavor! What body! What aroma! Full and rich . . . Jackson, my boy, this is terrific! I've tried them all. Some are pretty good. Most are horrible. The big trouble is, Jackson, that if a man likes the taste of coffee it's hard to get anything else to take the place of it. The substitutes don't have it. But this—if I didn't know, I might take this for coffee."

"Get used to it, it's not so bad," Jackson said.

"Would you mind giving Sister Jensen the recipe?"

"Well, sir, the house is in such a mess I don't know where I'd lay my hands on it right now."

The bishop chuckled. "You're a sly one, Jackson. You know very well this stuff is worth a fortune. The Saints would go wild over it. How about begging a little off you? I promise I won't examine it too closely."

"Tell the truth, Bishop, I'm a little low myself right now."

"Come, come, Jackson. I'm not trying to steal your formula. After all. And I'll keep it confidential if you wish. I understand how you must feel. You jumped like you'd been shot when I spoke at the door. Tell you what. I'm on my way to Wendover and I'll stop in on my way back for it. Now, I won't take no for an answer. Mix me up just a little bit. Couple of pounds or so."

"Well, sir, that's impossible," Jackson floundered. "You see, I've never been satisfied with it. Always thought I'd get around to improving it. You see, if . . ."

"It's plenty good enough for me."

"That's because you don't know what real coffee tastes like."

"Don't I?" the bishop said ruefully. "I used to be a great coffee hound as a young one. Before I went on my mission, of course. It's a taste you never forget. And there's nothing like a warm drink with a meal. Any doctor will tell you to drink a glass of hot water before breakfast. Tones up the system. I've tried them all. Fig-Coff, Barlo-Co, Coffee-Yum, and a dozen others. They don't have it." He extended his cup for a refill. "Delicious, Brother Jackson. Delicious. Coffee itself is hard on the nervous system."

"Certainly is," Jackson admitted, refilling the bishop's cup.

"The last time I had a cup of real coffee was when Katie was a baby. She was sick, and Sister Jensen and I were worn out. It was in January, and terribly cold, and I had to drive in to Wendover to get a prescription filled. I needed something to warm me up and keep me awake, so when I got to Wendover I got a cup of coffee in a cafe." The bishop wagged his head at the horrible memory. "Do you know, Brother Jackson, I didn't sleep a wink for four nights after that?"

"Good gosh," Jackson said, appalled.

"Not a wink for four nights. I twitched and tossed on a sleepless pillow. My nerves were on edge. My hands shook. It was a lesson to me."

Jackson wondered if a sick baby might not have had something to do with it; he hoped so, watching the bishop smack his lips over the second cup. "And maybe it was thinking about it made it worse," he suggested. "You knowed you'd done wrong and it preyed on you."

"Now, Brother Jackson," the bishop chided.

"Well?" a new voice said. Katie's face was at the hole in the door.

"Good grief," the bishop said. "Katie, I forgot you were waiting. Completely."

"I thought you were just dropping in for a second." Katie sniffed at the hole.

"Coffee-Near," the bishop said. "Got a drop left for her, Brother Jackson?"

"Sure."

"No, thanks. I'll wait in the car, Dad." Her face disappeared.

"Be right out!" the bishop called. His voice became confidential. "Brother Jackson, I just dropped into see how you felt about that—er—matter we talked of this morning. Any change in plans?"

"No, sir. I'm going to marry Katie, all right."

"You remember our discussion about proving yourself worthy?"

"Yes, sir."

"Brother Jackson, I feel different about things now than I did when we had that talk."

"Different, sir?" Jackson said apprehensively.

"I was inclined to be skeptical, Brother Jackson. I admit it frankly. There was a small seed of doubt in my mind. But now I know. I know that what you said was true. I know that your grandfather did appear to you with a message."

"Gee, that's swell, Bishop! I guess that about fixes things."

"Yes; I know, now. After you'd gone this morning I was troubled. I went to the Lord in prayer. I asked for guidance. And I in turn received a message. Brother Jackson, to prove yourself you must settle the Trouble."

"The Trouble? You mean, sir—the *Trouble?*"

"Yes, Brother Jackson. That was the message."

Jackson's jaw had sagged open. He never had expected a thing like this.

CHAPTER TWELVE

Jackson had been a very small boy at the time of the Trouble. While his memory might have dimmed, and his childish innocence at that time had prevented him from grasping the full implications, he grew up with it. The Trouble was still very much alive. Every so often a Church official would get up in Sunday meeting and tell the valley people they ought to be ashamed of themselves, that they ought to let the Spirit of the Lord lead them from such foolishness. It always sounded simple enough, but the thing had long since gone beyond reason and logic and kiss-and-make-up.

The square brick schoolhouse had always doubled as a place of worship. It was an economical arrangement, and nobody thought much about any change until one Sunday when Apostle Black was visiting. He got up to talk in meeting and said, "As I was coming through the valley I had a vision. I saw a fine new meetinghouse and beside it a lovely amusement hall for dances and socials, and a voice said to me, 'You will dedicate this place of worship for the valley.'"

Inasmuch as Apostle Black was at the time past sixty and in poor health there obviously was no time to lose. And the

Spirit of the Lord, people said, could be felt at the meeting. When Apostle Black sat down, Nephi Smith leaped to his feet and donated ten acres of good pasture land at the mouth of East Canyon for a site. Then Old Man Merrill Littlewall jumped up and pledged cement and gravel for a foundation that would last through the millennium. Old Man Merrill Littlewall was leader of the clan which lived at the south of the valley, and there was a considerable rivalry between the south and north, which had started originally as a squabble over water rights (the single creek ran from south to north; and water is gold in the desert), and had branched out into a quiet feud. Old Man Merrill Littlewall's pledge of the foundation put the heat on the north people, and Enoch Carter of the north end got up and pledged timber for the walls that would outlast the foundation.

It was a memorable meeting, and by its close everything had been pledged for a fine meetinghouse and amusement hall. Plans were drawn. Materials were hauled across the desert from Wendover. Apostle Black was due to arrive to dedicate the site. And then the Trouble began. The whole thing grew from the fact that Bessie Smith proved once again the truth of the old adage that love will find a way.

Nephi Smith, who'd donated the pasture land for a site, was a devout Saint, a widower with five beautiful daughters. His life had been saddened because four of his daughters had married outside the Temple. Two had run away with Gentiles, and twice he'd taken his .30-30 carbine, climbed into his Model T, and returned with a very scared young buck and the bishop to perform the ceremony. Folks said if Nephi's wife had lived the daughters might not have been wayward; but she hadn't and they had. They settled down after marriage to good honest wives and mothers.

With his youngest, Bessie, Nephi was strict. Bessie was a model girl. She taught Sunday school and was active in Mutual. She was pretty, but she never went out much because her father always went along too. Nephi Smith was determined that Bessie would be married in the Temple.

Nephi arrived at the bishop's place one evening with Bessie and young Ephraim Todd. Ephraim Todd was a wild one. He had drunk vanilla extract, Jamaica ginger, canned heat, and other odd substances before deciding to become his own source of supply; he was the valley bootlegger. And he was a Gentile.

"Bishop," Nephi announced, "these youngsters want to get married up. We come for a Temple recommend."

In the crook of his arm Nephi had his old .30-30.

The bishop cleared his throat.

"Ephraim here is willing to embrace the gospel," Nephi said. He glared at the white-faced young buck. "Ain't you, Eph?"

Ephraim nodded.

"He wants to go through the Temple . . . Don't you, Eph?"

Ephraim nodded.

"You want a recommend . . . Don't you, Eph?"

Ephraim nodded.

Bessie remained with downcast eyes.

The bishop again cleared his throat. "That's fine, Ephraim. I'm glad you're going to mend your ways and embrace the gospel. I'll baptize you next Fast Sunday, and then we'll see how things turn out. If you work hard in the faith I'm sure it won't be too long before you're an elder and we can talk about a recommend."

"We want that recommend now," Nephi said bluntly. "They're getting married right off."

"Oh," the bishop said.

"They can't wait," Nephi said.

"Brother Smith, I can't furnish a recommend under the circumstances."

"Yes, you can. Bishop, I lived a good life. And I never cut corners on my tithing like some. I've worked hard for the Church. And I donated ten acres of my best pasture land for the new meetinghouse."

"Brother Nephi, there isn't a better man in the valley than you are, nor one firmer in the faith. But you're not the one asking for the recommend."

"I am *too* asking for it!"

"You're not the one who's getting married. If these young people can't—if the situation is such—you can see how impossible the thing is."

"Bishop, it's been my life's ambition to have my daughters married up in the Temple. And Bessie is the onliest one I got left."

"Let us pray for guidance."

"I prayed myself black in the face. I want that recommend and I want it tonight. We're on our way to Salt Lake right now."

Ephraim and Bessie were married next day in Tooele by a justice of the peace. Ephraim never did join the Church.

Nephi Smith apostatized. If the Church couldn't do that

much for him in return for all he'd done, he said, to hell with the whole shebang. The title of the pasture land he'd donated was being searched, and when it came time for signing over the deed, Nephi said to hell with it. He'd pledged the land in a moment of religious hysteria, he said; go ahead and sue.

The site was piled with lumber and gravel and cement. Teams and scrapers were pledged to begin excavating the foundation as soon as Apostle Black arrived to dedicate the site. Apostle Black arrived and gave a spirited talk. There were miles and miles of land in this great valley, he said, that would do for a site. But he returned to Salt Lake without having dedicated one. The Trouble had already begun.

The Littlewall clan had decided to donate a nice site at the south end of the valley, a lovely site near the creek, with trees and all. The Carters had picked out a site down at the north end, the ideal place, the only place where a church house should really be.

Old Man Merrill Littlewall claimed that aside from everything else he was building the foundation and ought to have the say where it would go. The Carter faction scoffingly asked how much meeting you could hold in a foundation; the north end was the only place for their timber to stand.

The bishop, being centrally located, offered a compromise site. This might have been accepted, but for a pinto colt that was born on the Carter place with what might have been the letter *N* on its left shoulder. That, the north end claimed, was a sign. The south thereupon produced a carrot they'd dug up which was twisted somewhat like the letter *S*. A Carter boy and a Littlewall boy got into a fight at the schoolhouse dance. A Littlewall girl broke her engagement to a Carter boy (and both subsequently married unhappily). Sister Ormand, whose maiden name had been Carter, talked in tongues at a cottage meeting and, translating herself, said the Lord commanded the meetinghouse to be built on the north. Old Man Merrill Littlewall's wife had a dream in which a voice told her the church would be on the south site, and inasmuch as she had a stroke (her third) shortly afterwards, this was taken to be her dying testimony.

The thing was a cause. A man either had to be north or south. The only man in the valley who straddled the fence was the bishop, and both sides resented it. There was some talk of ousting him from the bishopric, except that even in the heat of the controversy everybody realized it was better to have some bishop than no bishop; the north and south would never be able to agree on his successor.

And meanwhile the lumber warped in the weather and the big pile of cement began to harden despite the protection of a tarp; gophers and rabbits made homes in the gravel.

The bishop, beyond his depth, called for help. Apostle Black arrived to bring the people to their senses. The apostle was late because it had begun to rain and his car got stuck in the desert. The storm, people felt, was a sign. It had been a dry year. Long Creek had dwindled to a bare trickle and irrigation was impossible. The crops were burning up; people felt they were being punished. Each side blamed the other for being mule-headed and bringing the wrath of God upon the valley.

Significantly, it was raining when Apostle Black arrived. Everybody gathered at the schoolhouse that afternoon hopeful and brimming with thanks and confident the site would either be north, or, on the other hand, south, depending upon where each came from.

It was a storm. As the opening hymn began there was a blinding flash and then thunder rocked the schoolhouse and darkness closed in as the rain came down in sheets. The thunder crashed again and again and the people sang louder and louder as if to appease an angry God, and the rain hit the roof like smashing breakers. It was a cloudburst. They'd wanted rain; they were getting it.

The gasoline lanterns were lighted, though it was still early afternoon. Water was standing on the ground between the brush hummocks outside, and the rain beat like hail at the windows. The bishop offered prayer, and Apostle Black got up to speak. He'd hardly got warmed up when the flood came boiling by.

The East Canyon watershed had been overgrazed for years, erosion had begun, and the dry year made things ripe for the cloudburst. One of the first bolts of lightning had struck the big pile of lumber at the mouth of the canyon. It was roaring in flame despite the rain when the wall of water, pushing trees and boulders before it, rolled down the canyon and scooped up the lumber and cement in passing.

When the storm was over, the ten-acre plot Nephi Smith had pledged and then taken back was a sea of boulders. The soil was stripped away and the land worthless. That, people said, was a sign, and it served him right. But the materials for the church were gone, too, the cement worthless, the gravel scattered, the lumber charred, broken, and warped, scattered over and buried under a dozen square miles of debris.

That was the Trouble. From that time on, any mention of building a meetinghouse was met in stony silence. If the Lord had wanted one built, people felt, He'd had His chance; He'd showed pretty definitely how He felt about things.

Old Nephi Smith had married again and had had one more daughter, Anita. She'd gone off to Salt Lake during the war and had returned with a fatherless baby. Let that be a lesson to apostates, people said; at least, before, his daughters had got married off somehow.

Apostle Black grew very old and very feeble.

And Jackson Skinner Whitetop, sitting on a box in his kitchen with a cup of coffee on his knee, regarded the bishop with something less than unrestrained joy.

"Me, sir?" he said croakingly. "*I* am to settle the Trouble?"

"Yes, Brother Jackson." The bishop put his empty cup on the floor and arose, patting his stomach comfortably. "A marvelous wholesome drink; marvelous. Don't forget; I'll pick up a little of it on the way back. Yes, Brother Jackson, a voice told me. You will settle the Trouble. And after that—well, we'll see." The bishop left, patting his stomach.

CHAPTER THIRTEEN

Jackson rummaged his memory for a recipe his mother had used one winter when the store had run out of coffee and the valley was snowed in. Let's see, there was burned barley, parched corn, scorched bread, egg shells, and just a couple of pinches of horse manure, as he remembered, to bring out the flavor. He browned the ingredients in a skillet, ground them in the old coffee mill, and made a cup of brew that was the color of sheep dip and tasted like the memory of original sin.

He discarded the experiment, and, adjusting the coffee grinder as tight as it would go, pulverized a half pound of coffee into which he'd put a few barley husks and an egg shell as camouflage. He put this in a fruit jar, pasted on a label, and wrote upon it *Coffee-Near*.

"In fact," he mused, "that is the nearest coffee the bishop ever drunk in his life."

When the bishop arrived that afternoon, Jackson took the fruit jar out to the car. Katie's greeting was casual, but her father beamed. "Fine, Brother Jackson! Fine! Do you have a minute?"

"All the time in the world."

"What say we go in and brew a cup of this delicious stuff? I've a matter to talk over with you."

"Well, all right," Jackson said, not too eagerly. The last little matter had saddled him with settling the Trouble and building a meetinghouse.

"I'll stay out here," Katie said firmly. "That house gives me the willies."

The bishop gave her a glance of reproving surprise, and followed Jackson into the kitchen. "What I don't know," Jackson said, pouring hot water into the coffee pot reluctantly, "is whether this Coffee-Near has got any bad effect on the system. Just a family recipe, you know. Never been tested."

"Nonsense, my boy. Nonsense. What possible harm from a brew of wholesome fruits and grains and berries? I drank two cups while I was here, and I never felt better in my life. Invigorating. My mind sharp as a bell. And on the way I got a marvelous idea. Brother Jackson, you've got something here, and I've taken the liberty of starting the ball rolling."

"Ball rolling?" Jackson said unhappily.

The bishop took the backless chair, and surveyed the kitchen reflectively. "Yes, it could be fixed up. The old log walls are still solid. Something to build on. Got your plans made?"

Jackson put coffee in the pot and set the pot on the edge of the stove. "I figured up a list of stuff I'd need, but I don't know when I'll get around to it. I seen Henry about what I had coming on the sheep. Instead of something coming, I owe him."

"Yes; poor Henry's had hard lick with the sheep."

"I owe him nine thousand dollars."

"Hmm. I didn't know it was as bad as that. Are your sheep worth that much?"

"I guess not, but Henry will take them and call it square." Jackson opened the lid of the coffee pot and regarded the brew with rapt attention while he spoke: "I've been wondering, Bishop. Inasmuch as I'm going to be your son-in-law, and the ranch here is good if it's run right, I been wondering if you'd like to advance some to fix it up on."

"Do you think a young fellow ought to get married under a load of debt?"

"Well, it depends on the prospects."

"True enough. But from a business standpoint the place is already mortgaged to the hilt."

Jackson had opened the door of the stove and stooped for a chunk of wood. He met the bishop's eye. "Mortgaged?" he asked in the tone of a man who has just been advised by his doctor that all these years a mistake has been discovered and he is not a man but a woman. "What mortgage?"

"The mortgage on the place here. That stove's smoking."

Jackson shoved in the wood and shut the stove door. "You mean this place is mortgaged?"

"I guess your folks weren't much of a hand to talk over business things with you. You remember the winter in Los Angeles? Let's see, when was that? Must be seventeen, eighteen years ago."

"You bet," Jackson said in fond memory. "I was only a kid, but I remember that. Palm trees, days on the beach . . ."

The bishop coughed. "On borrowed money. Your father came to me and said he wanted to buy that piece of hay land to the north of the place—the Carter field. Good investment. A man can't have too much hay. I advanced him the money and he changed his mind and spent the winter in Los Angeles."

"It was worth every dime they spent," Jackson declared. "The only vacation they ever really took. They never did quit talking about that winter in Los Angeles."

"It's over and done with now, Brother Jackson. My concern is the mortgage. Compound interest can be a terrible thing over the years. Your father never paid me a penny on principal or interest. I could have foreclosed, but what would your folks have done? I even paid the taxes to protect myself. It all adds up."

The bishop fished out a stub of pencil, looked around for paper, picked up an old magazine on the floor, wrote a figure on the margin, tore the figure off, and passed the scrap of paper to Jackson. "This is how things stand, including taxes for this year."

Jackson looked at the figure, turned the bit of paper over to see if he was reading the wrong side, and sat down on a box. "This is kind of sudden," he admitted.

"Do you think a man ought to plan on marriage when he's under a load of debt? It would be different if you had good prospects."

"Grandpa Skinner told me to. That's all I know."

"How's the brew coming?"

Jackson poured an extra cup for Katie and took it out to her. He was, he felt, reaping the wages of sin. He'd fed the bishop coffee, and coffee sharpens the mind. On the way to Wendover and back the bishop had seized upon this new obstacle to getting Katie.

Katie thanked him politely, took a bit of canned cream but no sugar, sipped, and said, "Coffee-Near? It certainly is near."

"You sound like an expert. What you wearing to the dance tonight?"

"I don't know. And what is that to you?"

"All right, if you want to surprise me. You'd look pretty in anything."

"If you're still twanging that string, Henry's taking me to the dance."

"I don't think so."

"That, of course, makes it different."

"You wait and see."

"You're awfully sure of yourself, Jack Whitetop."

"Got reason to be."

"Just why do you think I'd go with you?"

"Will you if Henry don't?"

"Of course he will."

"But if he don't?"

"Don't be silly."

"Then it's a date."

"It certainly isn't. Henry might be called away or something. In which case I'd go with my folks. I'm engaged, after all."

"I mean—if Henry goes to the dance but don't ask you, you'll go with me?"

"Why, certainly, Jack. And also if the moon comes up in the west and hell freezes over."

"Then it's a date."

"You are," she announced firmly, "the most insufferable conceited jackass . . ."

"Be seeing you," Jackson said fondly. While returning to the house, he took occasion to look again at the figure on the slip of paper. It looked just the same out here in the light— $14,771.11.

That was an awful lot of money. Particularly to be owing the man you hoped to persuade to be your father-in-law. And especially when you didn't know where your next dime was coming from.

The bishop was pouring himself another cup of coffee. "Things look dark now, Brother Jackson, but I'm sure it will all work out. Since receiving the message, I have great faith in you."

Jackson privately felt the bishop could go right on forever having inspirations that would make the marriage impossible. He didn't feel in a position to come right out and say so.

"How does Katie feel about your—er—proposition?" the bishop asked.

"She's thinking it over."

"True love never runs smooth, you know." The bishop sipped, and smacked his lips with gusto. He was in high good humor and, Jackson felt, had a right to be; he'd made conditions impossible, so why should he worry?

"About that little matter I wanted to speak to you about," the bishop said. "We got talking of other things, and then it's best to know where you stand before you talk business, anyhow."

"Matter?" Jackson said bleakly. What new bombshell?

The bishop chuckled. "Don't get excited. This is good news. That's why I saved it until the last. I got to thinking on the way to Wendover, and as soon as I got there I put in a long distance call to Salt Lake. Brother Jackson, the ball's rolling. I've always seen the possibilities for marketing a good coffee substitute among the Saints. Something really good would be a sensation. This stuff of yours is a gold mine. I have some connections in Salt Lake, and we've been looking for exactly this stuff you've been cooking up in your own kitchen. It's tentative, yet, of course—routine tests and all. But I'm not worried about that part of it, Brother Jackson. We've got the plant and distribution all lined up. I'll wager that in three weeks we're ready to roll. Inside of two months Coffee-Near will be on the breakfast table of every Saint in Utah. We'll push it. In six months . . ."

"But—you can't do that!" Jackson cried desperately.

The bishop slapped his leg and guffawed. "Here, here, my boy, don't get *that* idea about *me!* I'm not stealing it. That's what I'm here for. I lined the whole thing up on the phone. They'll go to work on that end, and my job is to close the deal with you. What do you think is fair, Jack?"

"Well, sir, it's just—well, impossible," Jackson said.

"I don't expect you to know the ins and outs of financing, manufacture, promotion—we'll take care of that, Jack."

"But you can't make it."

"I don't see why not, if you can stir it up in a kitchen."

"Well—it's got to be made in small batches," Jackson said, grasping any straw floating on the rising sea of his duplicity. "Funny thing. Make a half a pound, it's swell.

Try to make a pound batch and something happens. Couldn't possibly produce it in bulk."

"You just let the production men and chemists worry about that. They'll iron it out. I'm authorized to offer you two deals . . ."

"It wouldn't work out, sir. It's—awful expensive."

"Expensive?"

"Cost you five times as much as coffee."

"But you said it was made out of grains and berries."

"Yes, sir; but there's one ingredient that costs like the dickens."

"Then why do you drink it? It certainly hasn't been because of the Word of Wisdom. And anyhow, Jack, it's different buying things in bulk. This is all tentative; just a basis to work on. You can either take a royalty on every pound sold, or an interest in the company. Or some combination of the two."

"It isn't the price of it," Jackson foundered. "It's getting it that would cost. It's a desert weed. You might find one here, another a mile away. Awful scarce. You couldn't hire men to pick that weed and the stuff's no good without it."

"You show us the weed and I'll guarantee we can grow it under cultivation, Jack. Don't worry about the details. Let's just settle the broad picture now."

"Bishop, I'm sorry you went to all the trouble. I could of peddled the stuff myself, but it's impossible."

"Well, let's get down to cases. Where's the hitch?"

"I'd rather not talk about it, sir."

The bishop put his coffee cup on the floor and stood up. "You don't want to do business with me. Is that it?"

Jackson swallowed. "That's it."

"Well, it's your own affair. But I must say I'm mighty disappointed in you, Brother Jackson. Yes, mighty disappointed. Here's your chance to make something of yourself at last, and you turn it down flat. Good day, Brother Jackson."

Jackson wandered through the old house. Just this morning he hadn't had a worry in the whole world. Since Grandpa Skinner had appeared, every hour had heaped troubles on him. He paused before the crayon portrait of Grandpa Skinner.

"Well, Grandpa, what do I do now?"

The portrait glowered back silently. Grandpa Skinner was no bellhop to come at a call. He'd delivered his message once and for all. The only answer to Jackson's question was the scurrying of the mice overhead.

CHAPTER
FOURTEEN

Jackson drove south along the valley road in the early evening. He'd slicked down his hair, polished his boots, folded a blanket on the seat of the buckboard, curried his horses, greased the axles, shined the harness, and he was wearing his parachute-cloth muffler. He was all duded up to take Katie to the dance. All he needed was some idea of how to do it.

A gasoline lantern hung from the roof of the store porch. Cars were parked about; a wagon team and a saddle horse were at the hitching rack. The men were on the porch and the women inside shopping.

"Well, Romeo," Sid Worth said as Jackson gave a hitch of a halter rope to the pole.

The men were carefully grave; they were having fun.

"Hear you're getting married up, Jack," Young Merrill Littlewall remarked. Young Merrill's father, Old Man Merrill Littlewall, had been dead for years, but he'd always be Young Merrill, though he was crowding fifty and his hair was iron-gray.

"That's right," Jackson admitted.

"And taking Katie to the dance tonight," Reed Carter

said. Reed was now head of the Carter clan; his father, old Enoch, was feeble. "So they say."

"Why, sure. Sure, I'll take Katie to the dance."

The men exchanged sly glances.

"All duded up and ready to swing her high, wide, and handsome," Sid Worth observed.

"And what else you going to do?" Nephi Smith asked. Nephi had the only chair on the porch. He was along in his seventies, but his hair was black and his skin firm; his age was indicated by jutting eyebrows and a certain gnarled angularity. It had been a disappointment to many that Nephi Smith had held up so well after starting the Trouble and apostatizing. "Might as well clean up everything while you're about it."

"Sure, Jack," Sid Worth said. "No use being halfway about things."

"Oh, I ain't started yet," Jackson said. Gathered here were the representative factions of the Trouble—Nephi Smith, who'd started it, Reed Carter from the north end, and Young Merrill Littlewall from the south. The dry farmer, Sid Worth, was merely a gadfly who rode into the ground the fact that the truth can be uttered in jest. "Yep, before I'm done, we'll have a meetinghouse here in the valley. Me, I figure to settle the Trouble."

Every face stiffened; the heavy playfulness was gone. The Trouble was something you didn't joke about.

"And what's more—"

"Let it ride, Jack," Reed Carter said.

"We was just horsing," Young Merrill Littlewall said. "You don't have to get hostile."

Sid Worth kept discreetly silent. Even a jester knew there were some things you didn't bring up.

"I'm not hostile and I'm not horsing," Jackson said. "I said I was going to settle the Trouble, and that's what I meant."

In the silence, the slap of Sid Worth's hand against his hip was like a shot. "*He's* going to settle the Trouble!" Sid cried. "Well, if Jack Whitetop says it, then I reckon it's official!" Sid followed his own cue with a loud guffaw. The other men waited uncertainly, watching the reactions of Nephi Smith, Reed Carter, and Young Merrill Littlewall. Nephi slapped a gnarled hand on the chair arm.

"Yep, that settles it!" Nephi roared.

Then everybody laughed. "Jack, you're a card!" Reed Carter cried.

"Anything for a laugh!" Young Merrill laughed.

Sid Worth, very satisfied with himself for having turned it all off as a joke, nodded encouragingly to Jackson, indicating that Jackson should also join the fun.

Jackson scowled. He was filled with unreasoning resentment towards all the Carters, Smiths, and Littlewalls. If they hadn't started the Trouble in the first place, he wouldn't be saddled with settling it.

"You just wait and see!" he declared furiously. They laughed the louder. It was so ridiculous, the valley trash shooting off his face about what he was going to do. The guffaws brought the women to the door. Milo Ferguson edged through them onto the porch, scowling as he made furious clouds of cigar smoke. Henry Brown pulled in; he'd been over to the schoolhouse helping shave candles and spread cornmeal on the floor for dancing.

"Hey, Henry," Sid Worth called. "Guess what Jack Whitetop is going to do now, besides take your girl away from you?"

Henry climbed out of the weapons carrier, grinning. "What?"

"Now he's going to settle the Trouble! He's going to build us a meetinghouse, personal!"

Henry Brown threw back his head and roared. He doubled, beating his fist on his leg, and then grabbed his back and straightened slowly. "Jack, you're killing me. If I throw out my sacroiliac on account of you . . . Jack, you dog!"

"Hey, Jack," Reed Carter said. "Are you going to build the meetinghouse afore or after you take Katie to the dance?"

That was good for another whoop, and Sid Worth, feeling a bit put out 'cause he hadn't thought of it, knitted his brows for another crack.

"Laugh, you dang jackasses!" Milo Ferguson yelled. "Go ahead and laugh! But I'll tell you something! If Jack Whitetop says he'll settle the Trouble, then he *will*."

"Well, if you say so, Milo," Young Merrill Littlewall drawled.

"That makes it official," Sid Worth said.

The laughter echoed again. But old Nephi Smith turned in his chair to cock an eye at Milo. Being the only two apostates in the valley, Nephi and Milo had considerable in common. They liked to get together to cuss out the gospel, and they had mutual respect for each other's good judgment. "Why for you say that, Milo?"

"I'll tell you why, if you'll shut up a second!"

"Let's get this," Sid Worth said. "It ought to be good."

The group paused expectantly. Milo spat deliberately. "Yes, I'll tell you why. On account of Jackson's grandfather appeared to me today in spirit form. Old Moroni Skinner . . ."

"Milo," Jackson said, "you better shut up."

"I won't shut up for you or nobody looks like you. Anyhow, Moroni Skinner appeared to *me* and I got a right to talk about what happens to me. Yep, Moroni Skinner talked to me today. Just like anybody else. I was sitting here on the porch this morning and he appeared and talked to me just like I'm a-talking to you."

"Moroni Skinner," Nephi said. "Well, doggone! Say, how was the old coot?"

"Just like he used to be. Even looked younger, but he said that was on account I was older."

"How'd you know it was him?"

"How do I know you're Nephi Smith?"

"Hell, there ain't no such of a thing as a spirit," Nephi said. "You know that."

"Sure, I know it. But it was Moroni Skinner, all right, with his chin whiskers and that black hat, all dressed up for Sunday. He talked with me awhile and then he disappeared. Right afore my very eyes. Here one second and gone the next. Standing right there on the porch. Funniest thing ever happened to me."

"Hell, you're an apostate," Nephi Smith said. "If there *was* any such of a thing as a spirit, they wouldn't be appearing to *you*."

"I was sort of surprised, myself," Milo admitted. "Especially how it happened. How it happened, I was sitting here thinking. I was thinking how happy I was to know the gospel for the pack of superstitious lies it was . . ."

"Take it easy, Milo," Young Merrill Littlewall said. "You're welcome to your beliefs but don't go running down ours."

"Don't get touchy, Merrill. I'm just a'telling you how it was. I was sitting here thinking such happy thoughts and all of a sudden there he was. Old Moroni Skinner. Plain as the nose on your face. And a-talking to me just like I'm talking to you." Milo puffed at his cigar with satisfaction.

"Well?" Reed Carter said. "What did he say?"

"That there's none of your affair. What a spirit tells you is personal."

"Sure did reform you," Young Merrill observed dryly, looking at the cigar.

"Hell, I'm an apostate. I don't believe in spirits," Milo said. "He wasn't here on my account. He come to see young Jackson here, and while he was down he sort of dropped by to tell me a couple of things, too." Milo turned to Jackson. "What message did he give you, Jack?"

"I don't know what you're talking about," Jackson snapped. "And anyhow, you talk too damned much."

"If it's sacred to you, it's all right by me," Milo said. "Don't get hostile. Me, I can take a visitation or I can leave it alone. If you don't want to talk, it's your business. But if Moroni Skinner didn't want it to get around, he had no business appearing to *me*. I never made him no promises, and I don't believe in that stuff anyhow. Spirits! Visitations!

Pack of nonsense! Why didn't the old fool leave me alone? I was happy the way I was."

"As happy as if you had good sense," Sid Worth agreed.

"Rats!" Nephi Smith cried, his jutting eyebrows lowering. "A man like you, Milo! A good, honest apostate, and first thing you know you're having visitations!"

"Don't *you* go jumping on me, Nephi Smith! I can cuss the gospel out with anybody! Moroni didn't do no preaching to me, and what happened don't change my mind about nothing. But whether I believe in such stuff or not don't cut no ice—it *happened*."

Nephi's youngest daughter, Anita, smiled prettily at Milo. "There must be some things that he said which you can repeat."

"Well," Milo said. A man is never too old to be softened by a pretty smile. "I don't reckon it was so very secret . . ."

"Milo, you shut up," Jackson said.

"I won't shut up! I'll tell you what he told me. Moroni Skinner he told me he was down here on earth to straighten Jackson out. Now, what he told Jackson, I don't know . . ."

"I haven't never said he appeared to me," Jackson pointed out.

"Are you denying it?"

"I'm not saying."

"Ha!" Milo cried. "Then he *did!* Well, it's your affair, Jack. What your grandfather told you is between you and him. But something sure did change you in a hurry, Jack. Wasn't long after Moroni appeared to me that you come driving down the road and told me you was fixing to marry Katie Jensen. And now it's settling the Trouble. You ain't the same young buck you was yesterday, Jack. Something's put fire on your tail." Milo glared about at the people on the porch. "The rest of you jackasses can go ahead and laugh. Laugh and be damned. But you'll laugh out of the other side of your mouth when it happens. From now on, when Jack Whitetop here says a thing is going to be, why, me, I'm listening!"

CHAPTER
FIFTEEN

Milo turned and went inside the store. "Rats!" Nephi
Smith cried. "Spirits! Visitations! Never heard such tommy-
rot in my born life!" But the apostate's reaction was strictly
his own. The others were troubled and sobered. They'd
been raised in the tradition of visitations. It was particularly impressive that Moroni Skinner had appeared to a
disbeliever such as Milo.

Young Merrill Littlewall ran a hand through his iron-
gray hair. He said quietly, "Jack, is it anything you can talk
about?"

Jackson shrugged. "Wish the old fool had kept his big
mouth shut."

"We understand, Jack," Reed Carter said.

Anita Smith crossed the porch and took Jackson's arm.
"Can I talk to you a minute?" They went around the store
together.

It was a small enough incident, and would have passed
unnoticed at any other time. But now that Jackson's
strange behavior of the day was explained, nothing he
could do was in any way small; it was all part of a pre-
ordained pattern.

Reed Carter put the feeling into words: "Hear tell Apostle Black is mighty low. They don't expect him to live."

This, significantly, was the first time in a decade or more that anybody from the north had made reference to the Trouble within earshot of anybody from the south.

"Something better happen pretty quick," Sid Worth said. "I hear they expect him to pass on any day now."

"Well, it's in the open now and I'm glad of it," Young Merrill Littlewall said. "When things are so bad that a spirit has to appear to an apostate—well, what does that make *us?*"

"I feel ashamed of myself," Reed Carter admitted. He and Young Merrill regarded each other tentatively.

"Go ahead, you two," Sid Worth said. Sid was a man who couldn't keep out of anything, even the Trouble. "Shake hands. Nothing which can't be settled by man-to-man discussion."

"I guess that's it," Young Merrill admitted. "We just been trying to hide the thing."

"I'm willing to talk it over if you are," Reed Carter admitted.

They shook hands warmly. "Isn't it terrible how we let a thing like that fester?" Young Merrill said.

"I feel better a'ready," Reed said.

"Why don't we get together and settle the whole thing right now? We still got that site up in the south end. Why don't we start the ball rolling at the dance tonight? We can be staking the site off in the morning."

"Merrill, that's a good idea and I'm with you a thousand percent. As a matter of fact we already got it staked off down in the north end. I still got a copy of those old plans, and I've had the north site all staked off and ready to go for years."

"Where'd you get a copy of the plans?"

"Never mind. We got 'em and we're ready to go. What say, Merrill?"

"You been pretty sure of yourself," Young Merrill said.

"Why not? We just been a-waiting for something like tonight to happen."

"I don't think I like it."

"What don't you like?"

"You folks in the north has just been laying in the weeds waiting."

"I don't think I like *that*," Reed Carter said. "We're just trying to build a place of worship. And we'd had it up years ago if some people in this valley wasn't mule-headed like a jackass. Nothing personal, Merrill."

"Any fool knows there's only one place to put that meetinghouse," Young Merrill said. "Not mentioning no names, but if some folks from the north didn't have their minds closed shut like a steel trap, they'd seen it long ago."

The others quietly drifted into the store, leaving Young Merrill and Reed Carter, voices rising, to argue around and around. The Trouble had only had the scab picked off.

Henry Brown stood beside the store filled with doubts and vague fear. Jackson and Anita had gone out behind, and Henry was afraid of what she might tell him. Henry Brown was, in truth, a pagan, with all the vague and unformalized superstition of a man without a cut-and-dried faith to cling to. He was a Saint for the sake of expediency. He gave the gospel lip service, and at times he felt guilty and a bit afraid. If there *was* anything to the gospel, where would he come off? Of course there wasn't, but what if there was? A hypocrite was worse than an apostate. He'd become a Saint because it was the only way to get Katie. And he'd worried more than he liked to admit whether it would affect his luck. He prided himself on his business sagacity, but, deep down, Henry Brown considered it luck. What if it turned on him? He had on occasion paid a little income tax which he might have concealed. He had wiped out the store bill, on occasion, of men who'd had a disastrous year. He had made a practice of donating the candles and cornmeal for the schoolhouse floor for dances. He'd told himself that by being active and prominent in the local church he was helping others live better. He always gave an expensive present when anybody got married in the valley. This had given him the reputation of a generous man, and he like to fancy himself such. He didn't realize he was offering sacrifices to the goddess luck.

Vague fear of unknown forces gripped him as he waited for Jackson and Anita to reappear from behind the store. His affair with Anita in Salt Lake had been something of the moment. He'd washed his hands of it after doing the right thing. But it had proved persistent, and the child she'd brought back was developing horribly to look like him. Henry shook off his fears. Damn Milo! Shooting off his face about visitations! The old fool! Getting feeble in his old age. Seeing ghosts. Pack of nonsense.

Behind the store, Anita looked up at the sky. "What lovely stars!"

"They're O.K."

"And what a wonderful moon!"

"Hard to beat," Jackson said. "Did you want to see me about something?"

"Oh, I just wanted to tell you how happy I am that everything's settled."

"What is?"

"About you marrying Katie and all. Isn't it marvelous to know you have nothing to worry about?"

"You seem pretty sure about it."

"Aren't you? Don't tell me you're doubting a message from beyond."

"I never said I had any message."

"You don't have to. We thought you were touched the way you acted today, but what Milo said clears it up. I just wanted to say how happy I am, Jack."

"I appreciate it," Jackson said, baffled. Just why Anita Smith should be happy about it was too much for him. "That all?"

Anita laughed. She was a saucy girl, and some folks wondered how she could keep up her spirits under the load of her disgrace; she carried the disgrace as if it were a feather.

"Well, if it works out for you it will for me," she said.

"What will?"

"You wait and see. Should we go back?"

"O.K."

She took his arm again. "Jack, you're going to take Katie to the dance tonight. Wait and see."

"I got to make Henry step aside, somehow."

"He will." There was devilment in her eyes.

"Why?"

"Because I said so. Wait and see."

Jackson was puzzled. From all outward appearances, Anita had had private words of great importance with him. Yet she'd merely talked of the moon and stars and said she was happy things would turn out. Didn't make sense. As they returned, Henry was waiting beside the store.

"Jack, I'd like a word with you."

"Certainly, Henry," Anita said. "Now, Jack, remember your promise! Not a word!" And she skipped onto the porch before Jackson could ask her what promise and what word.

"What'd she say to you?" Henry demanded.

"Just wanted me to look at the stars."

"The stars."

"And the moon."

"I asked you a question. Do I look like a half-wit?"

"As a matter of fact, Henry, I've always figured you for a very smart hombre."

"Oh," Henry said. This, then, was a threat. "Don't worry, I'll do the smart thing," he said. "O.K., I'm listening."

"That's all," Jackson said. "Except she said she was glad everything was going to work out for me and her."

"Oh, she said that."

"And she said you'd step aside and let me take Katie to the dance."

"Look here, Jack Whitetop," Henry said dangerously. "Do you think you can scare me?"

"Hate to try it," Jackson admitted frankly. "I'm just telling you what she said. You wanted to know."

Henry changed his mood abruptly. He chuckled. "Jack, why for are we getting stirred up? Of course there's not a word of truth in her story. Not a word. But I've humored her. I feel sorry for her, for one thing. After all, she'd had a hard time of it."

"I sort of admired her, myself," Jackson said. "Coming back here with the baby and facing people she knew. She could of stayed away."

"And you see how it is with me, Jack. A man in my position. Engaged to Katie, and in the bishopric. In the public eye. I've tried to help her, and she's got the wrong idea. I don't want to make any trouble for her."

"Why, sure, Henry," Jackson said.

Henry studied the younger man, uncertain as to whether Jackson was as innocent as he appeared or deeper and shrewder than he had a right to be.

"But we got off the track, Jack. What I really wanted to see you about, I was wondering if you'd do me a little personal favor. I'd appreciate it, Jack."

"All depends, Henry."

"It just come to me. I've been so doggone busy and excited I clean forgot poor Whitey Jones. Can you beat that? I wonder if you'd take my sedan and go pick up Katie and her folks. I'll go out to the herd and pick up Whitey in the weapons carrier. Would you do that for me, Jack? I'd sure appreciate it. Tell Katie I'll be in a little later. Put your horses in my stable and take my sedan. Would you do that for me, Jack?"

"Well, I reckon I can help you out, Henry," Jackson admitted. "When you put it that way. You can do something for me sometime." Sure was amazing how things were working out. Yes, sir.

CHAPTER SIXTEEN

Katie opened the door at Jackson's knock, smiling in anticipation. She was lovely in a long white evening dress. "We're all ready; come on in!" she said gaily; then she recognized Jackson and said, "Oh." She turned to her parents, who were seated in the living room wearing wraps and hats. "It's Jackson. I guess he wants to see you, Dad."

"Come in, Brother Jackson," the bishop said. "We're just leaving. Expecting Henry any minute now."

"I come in his place. He asked me wouldn't I come and pick you all up."

"He what?" Katie said sharply.

"He said it would be a personal favor if I'd take you to the dance."

"Oh, he did, did he? I'll let *him* tell me that."

"He asked me to take his sedan and pick you folks up. I told him I'd oblige."

The bishop crossed to the front window, cupped his hands at his face, and peered at the car outside. "Henry all right?"

"Henry's fine. Fit as a fiddle," Jackson said.

"I don't understand it," Sister Jensen said emphatically.

"He said he had to go pick up Whitey Jones at the herd and bring him in to the dance."

"Whitey ain't crippled," the bishop said. "He's got his own rig."

"Whitey's more important than I am," Katie said.

"Why didn't you go out and pick up Whitey?" Sister Jensen asked.

"He didn't ask me to."

"It beats me," the bishop admitted. "Well, let's go. Ready, Ma? . . . Katie, get your things on . . . Jackson, you're a deep one. I'm just beginning to realize it."

"I'm just doing Henry a favor," Jackson said virtuously.

"I'm going to give Henry a talking to and he won't forget it," Sister Jensen said. "A-sending just anybody. Is this the way he'll treat her after they're married?"

"They ain't going to get married, ma'am," Jackson said.

"Oh, yes, they are. And if Henry and Katie *didn't* get married, I'd sooner see myself in the grave than let her marry trash like you."

"Turning off a bit chilly tonight," the bishop said diplomatically. "Changed your mind on that matter we talked about this afternoon, Brother Jackson?"

"No, sir. I don't really believe we ought to mix business and family relationships."

"What's this?" Sister Jensen asked.

"Nothing you'd be interested in, Ma," the bishop said. "I made Jackson a little business proposition."

"I certainly wouldn't do business with that trash."

"I ain't trash," Jackson said. "Not any more. I reformed."

Sister Jensen sniffed. Katie came in with her coat on and

they went out to the car. The bishop and his wife got in the back. "Plenty of room back here, Katie," Sister Jensen said.

"I'll ride with my escort," Katie said, getting in beside Jackson. "If Henry thinks he can send a pinch hitter, he can think again."

"Well, I never," Sister Jensen said.

The bishop said nothing; he seemed resigned to forces beyond his control.

The schoolhouse was a square structure of red brick sitting in a brushed-off clearing of the sage flat. The bishop's party arrived between dances, and there was momentary silence and then a buzz of conversation as everybody saw Katie coming in with Jackson. Anita Smith grinned saucily from the bench on the north wall. The stag group was near the big wood-burning stove in the corner next to the door, and Henry's camp mover, Whitey Jones, was large as life there.

"Where's Henry?" Katie asked Whitey Jones.

"Henry? Ain't seen him since this morning. He brought Mack out this morning and picked up Ned Holt . . ."

"Henry went out to pick you up and bring you in to the dance," Jackson broke in helpfully. "Did you miss him?"

Whitey's eyes shifted. "Why—yes, I guess I missed him."

"You must of forgot he was coming out to pick you up."

"Yes, that's right. I plumb forgot."

"Never mind prompting him, Jack," Katie said. "Will you take my coat in the other room for me?"

The school desks had been piled high in a corner of the south room. A table had been set up and the older women were already fixing things for the midnight dinner. Babies were parked about, and kids lurked as near as they dared to the table, ready to snatch something and run. Jackson put the coat on a desk.

"You've got him," Anita said, arriving apparently to look at her sleeping child. "Make him squirm." Her eyes twinkled. "He's furious!"

"Why have I got him?"

The music began and Anita hurried into the north room. Jackson went in and claimed Katie. "First and last dance for your escort."

"And every third one between," Katie agreed. "He can't do this to me!"

"Have you thought it over yet?"

"Are you still harping on that string? You played some low trick on him. I know you. If I was Henry I'd take you out back and give you the licking of your life."

"If you was Henry you'd stay healthy and not try it. And if you was Henry I wouldn't be dancing with you."

"Poor Henry."

"I ain't done nothing to Henry. I'm doing him a favor, is all."

"I'll bet he appreciates it. You pulled some vile trick on him and don't deny it. I've heard this talk about Milo Ferguson's visitation."

"It sure gets around. I wasn't in the other room half a minute."

"Wishful was at the store tonight. Somehow you've played on Henry's faith. I know it. He's a religious man and you're taking advantage of it. That's a low trick, Jack."

"It sure would be, if I done it."

"Did your grandfather really appear to you, Jack?"

"That's not for me to say."

"You don't deny it. It's pretty low to use a thing like that to influence Henry."

Jackson didn't argue; it was enough to have Katie near him.

He went outside for the next two dances, savoring the memory of the formalized embrace. It was unthinkable to take another girl in his arms between dances with Katie. When he danced with her again she refused to say anything at all, and kicked him deftly on the ankle when he tried to draw her close. Then suddenly she was against him, smiling prettily and laughing with gay abandon, and he saw that Henry had come in with Ned Holt and Beulah Hess. Henry glowered across the dance floor, and Beulah glowered. Ned Holt alone seemed happy at having cut Jackson out with Beulah for the evening.

Henry was crossing the floor almost before the music stopped. "Why, hello, Henry," Katie said. "I didn't expect you for hours, and I'm filled up for the next six dances . . . Jack, third one from this, remember!"

Beulah Hess was near the outside door, waiting. Her cheeks were white, throwing the lip rouge into vivid relief. The Hesses were famous in the valley for temper, and Jackson had no desire to face Beulah when she was riled up. With her at the doorway he either had to ask somebody to dance or face her, and it was unthinkable to dance with anybody but Katie. He wondered why he'd ever gone out with Beulah anyhow.

As the music began he slipped through the connecting door to the south room and hurried past the long table and outside. He was slipping around the corner of the schoolhouse when a feminine voice cried, "Jack!" But then, Jack was a common name. A girl couldn't follow out back; that was man's territory.

Milo Ferguson was sitting on the rock rim of the well. From the shed behind the schoolhouse came muted sounds of young bloods slyly experimenting with the foul deceiver. Jackson hitched onto the well beside Milo.

"Wished I knew, Jack," Milo said. He seemed to be puffing even more furiously than ordinarily on his cigar. "Yep. Wished I knew why old Moroni Skinner appeared to me, is what I can't figure out. Must of been connected with you somehow. But the old fool might of told me what."

"Maybe you needed some saving yourself," Jackson suggested.

Milo snorted. "I made up my mind about the gospel, and to hell with it. Anyhow, Moroni wouldn't of come to see me about myself. He said he was here on account of you. Henry's sore."

"I expect he is."

"What'd you tell him, to get his car and his girl?"

"He asked me to do it as a favor."

"He sure appreciated it, too. Ripped into me after you'd gone. Said I should of kept my mouth shut about my visitation. As if it was *his* business. I had that visitation and I'll talk about it as much as I damned please. Might of lost my job except Henry don't know what I . . ." Milo checked himself, and then said, "Except you can't fire a man for having a visitation. Not in this country."

Jackson wondered what the old man had almost said.

Milo rolled his cigar reflectively between his lips. "Jack, did Moroni tell you about Henry Brown?"

"I haven't said he told me anything."

"Why don't you quit talking like a blamed fool? Everybody knows he did!"

"What about Henry?"

"He must of done. You put the squeeze on Henry and he stepped aside tonight. Damned near time somebody did. Me, it's none of my business. Shut up," he said as Henry appeared around the schoolhouse.

Henry crossed to the well. "Any trouble, Jack?"

"Trouble? What kind?"

"Car run O.K. and everything?"

"Sure. Why not?"

"I appreciate you helping me out, Jack."

"You sure do," Milo said acidly.

"Beulah wants to see you, Jack."

"I don't want to see Beulah."

"She's out in the car, Jack. You'd better see her. You know these Hess people when they get riled. You can't blame her much. You've been going with her pretty steady. You better have a little talk with her anyhow."

"What car?"

"Your car, Jack. The sedan's yours for tonight. Use it all you want so long's you're back in the morning. Don't do anything I wouldn't do."

"Henry," Milo said, "you're entirely too blamed happy."

Jackson crossed to the cars parked before the schoolhouse. Beulah was in Henry's sedan. "Get in, Jack," she said, and he got in resignedly. He knew what was coming.

When Beulah was riled up she had to get it off her chest, and then she was all right. She'd got her temper from her father, Ross Hess, who, according to local legend, had once taken an ax to a balky horse and in a fit of temper had thrown a wheelbarrow right through the wall of his front room. Ross Hess was ordinarily a mild little man, who wouldn't tip the scales at a hundred and fifty. He'd bought a piano on the installment plan, and a dunning letter so enraged him that he'd picked up the piano bodily and flung it out the door, without opening the door; and then, the fury over, had sat down calmly to write the company to come and get it, adding an apologetic P.S. that he was sorry it had got a bit scratched in an unavoidable accident. He was always very sorry after an outburst.

Beulah didn't throw things. She scratched. She got her gripe off her chest, and then her voice suddenly went up a notch and she scratched. Jackson sat quietly, listening not to what she said so much as to the tone of voice, ready when it rose, to grab her hands. It generally didn't last long, and she was always so sorry afterwards.

She went on at some length about what a dirty-pants, two-timing, chiseling heel he was, going with her and keeping other fellows away, and now throwing her over and making a fool of himself over Katie Jensen. He wasn't particularly listening, for her voice hadn't risen. Then she said, "All right, sit there. If you don't think so, sit there!" He glanced at her, and then quickly averted his face.

Beulah was wearing an aqua dress fastened at the front with three large buttons above the waist. She'd undone two of the buttons and slipped the dress from one shoulder.

"Hey, what are you doing?" he said.

"I told you what I was doing. You led me on and you're going to be a man about it. Or do you want me to scream?"

Jackson was puzzled. Her voice hadn't risen. "What is this? Say, somebody's been talking to you."

"All right, what if he did? It's the truth, isn't it? You can't lead me on and then drop me like an old shoe!"

"Henry's been talking to you."

"All right, and what of it? We're driving to Tooele tonight and we'll get married." She pulled the dress from her other shoulder. "Or should I scream?"

"You better cover yourself up," he said. "You won't scream."

"Oh, won't I? You just think I won't."

"We couldn't get old enough to live a thing like that down. Not in this valley. Look at Nephi Smith's girls and how long it's been. You won't scream."

"I hate you!" she cried, her voice suddenly rising to that critical pitch. She clawed his cheek before he caught her arms. She always had a brief surge of terrible strength, and Jackson was wrestling for dear life when he suddenly was jerked backwards out of the car onto the seat of his pants and he couldn't see what was going on for warding off a flurry of fists.

"Get up!" Ned Holt said eventually, pausing for breath. "Get up and fight like a man, you dog!"

Jackson lowered his arms cautiously. A circle had formed already and people were running from the schoolhouse crying, "Fight! Fight!"

"Ned!" Beulah cried. Her passion was gone and she was terribly contrite. She also was in a bad position.

"It's all right, darling," Ned said protectingly. "Lucky I got here just in time . . . This dirty skunk attacked her!" he announced to the circle at large. "Tearing off her dress! When I got here she was fighting for her honor!"

Beulah burst into loud wails.

"Get up!" Ned cried to Jackson. "Get up and fight like a man!"

CHAPTER
SEVENTEEN

Jackson had no desire to get up. He was fifteen years younger than Ned Holt and a head taller, and he had no ill feeling at a natural mistake.

"You got it all wrong," he said. "Beulah and me was just having a little talk."

"Oh!" Beulah sobbed. She clung to Ned Holt, weeping. She could hardly admit she'd made a fool of herself. She had been only a tool for Henry, she saw. And, too, Ned Holt's bravery in jumping a man twice his size had touched her tender little heart. She hadn't known Ned had the spunk. Why, he was positively gorgeous! Reminded her a lot of her father in a rage.

"I wouldn't marry him if he was the last man in the world!" she declared.

"What?" the bishop said, startled, from the circle of spectators. Jackson saw Katie in the crowd, eyes wide and unbelieving. Henry Brown had the expression of a cat who has just polished off a fat mouse.

"Get up and take your whipping!" Ned Holt yelled, trying to disengage himself from Beulah's embrace.

"Let him alone, Ned," Bishop Jensen said.

"You don't want to see this, Katie," Henry said, taking her arm.

"Jack, I guess you'd better go and keep on going," the bishop said.

Young Merrill Littlewall spoke up. He was smarting from the fracas with Reed Carter at the store. "He ought to be horsewhipped," he declared.

"We'll see you do the right thing by her," Reed Carter said.

"Like hell you will!" Ned Holt cried. "Why do you think I saved her for?"

Beulah burst into a loud wail. "Ned, you're so wonderful!" She'd threatened just such a scene, but the last thing she'd wanted was for it to happen.

"You better come along with us, Jack," Reed Carter said.

The bishop raised a hand. "Leave him alone. It's enough punishment, the whole valley knowing what kind of man he is."

"That's all right, Bishop," Ned Holt said. "But we can't just let a man go around attacking innocent girls. The sheriff will handle this. This is something for the law."

"Sheriff?" Nephi Smith scoffed. The old man lifted a gnarled fist. "In my day we knowed how to handle a thing like this without no sheriff."

Milo stood puzzled; his cigar had gone out.

"You want to swear out a complaint, Sister Beulah?" the bishop asked.

"Oh, no, no, no! It was all—I want to forget everything!"

"I understand," the bishop said quietly. "Men, we don't want to drag a decent girl's name in the mire. I want all of you to forget this thing. It's the girl's good name we must think about. The reputation of an innocent girl is a priceless thing."

"You're off the track a mile, Bishop," Nephi said. "The girl wasn't hurt. It's this here—this fiend here that we're thinking about."

"He'll leave the country, I'll guarantee that," the bishop said. "And never come back."

"We don't need your guarantee," Nephi said. "We'll take care of that."

"I guess we know what to do," Reed Carter said.

"What we waiting for?" Young Merrill Littlewall asked. Young Merrill and Reed Carter were a solid front in one respect, at least; they'd cooperate against anybody or anything trying to stir up the Trouble.

"Wait, men," the bishop said pleadingly. He'd heard about the fracas Jackson had caused at the store with his remark about settling the Trouble. And the bishop, even though he'd heard it as a message from beyond, felt a bit responsible. "The greatest test of character is to forgive. Let's be big about this. I'm sure Jackson lost his head. You all know he's been acting strangely. Perhaps he'll need medical attention. I'll take him to a doctor."

"You just stand by, Bishop," Nephi Smith said. "When we're done, he'll need a doctor."

"He's got to have a lesson he'll never forget," Young Merrill Littlewall said indignantly. "Personally, I'm all for trying to forgive and forget. But it wouldn't be right to Jackson to let him off scot-free."

"There's other innocent girls we got to think about,"

Reed Carter said, just as virtuously. "We can't just turn him loose on them."

"In a way we're doing him a kindness, teaching him a lesson," Young Merrill said roundly.

"I hate to do it, personally," Reed Carter said. "But we got to, for his own good."

"Yeah, it hurts me worse'n it does him," Nephi declared. "But what we palavering for? Where'd Henry go? He's got some tar down at the store."

"I got sheep dip," Young Merrill suggested.

"Just as good," Reed Carter said. "We can use the hitching pole here at the schoolhouse for a rail."

"Get up on your feet, Jack," Young Merrill said. "Take it like a man."

"Oh, no, no, no!" Beulah wailed. "Don't hurt him! It's all my fault!"

"Ned, take care of your woman," Nephi said.

Jackson got up and brushed off his pants. If there were any more visitations being passed around from now on, he felt he'd just as soon be left off the list. Never a bit of trouble all his life. He'd always got along with people. Everybody had liked him, if they didn't respect him. And now in one single day look what he'd got himself into. Here were men he'd known all his life ready to snatch him away and ride him out of the valley on a rail. If Grandpa Skinner had just minded his own business and left him alone, he would have been all right.

"Bishop," Young Merrill Littlewall said quietly, "you'd better go on inside. And all the women clean out of here. This is a dirty job and the men will handle it."

"Men!" the bishop cried. "Please! Don't do anything in haste you'll live to regret!"

It was too late for talk. He was shouldered aside. The mob fused into a unit, the individual mind melting in the mass. The mass swarmed over Jackson, tossed him overhead and carried him to the hitching pole. The pole screaked from its sockets, and Jackson, straddling it, was born aloft.

"Wait! Wait! You can't do that!"

Anita Smith rushed into the mob, her sleeping child clutched to her chest.

"Nita, you take that baby and git out of here," Nephi told his daughter.

Anita lifted her child high to the man on the rail. "Here, Jack. Kiss the little dear good-by. You may never see him again."

"Huh?" Jackson said blankly.

The mob stopped, curious.

"What's this, Nita?" her father said suspiciously.

"Let me up there with him," Anita said nobly. "Ride us both out on a rail. All three of us. Where he goes, we go. His people are our people."

"What's he got to do with you?" Young Merrill Littlewall asked.

"I think I know," Reed Carter said. There was a general lifting of eyebrows.

"Nita," old Nephi said, his jutting eyebrows lowering, "tell me the truth. Is the coyote I've been a-looking for sitting up there on that pole?"

"Dad, don't ask me that question!" Nita cried, lowering her eyes demurely.

"Well I'll be, go to hell!" Nephi cried. "I'll be dipped in mud! Daughter, why didn't you tell me this afore?"

"Oh, Dad, you wouldn't ask me to marry this lazy trash!"

"Is he the father of that brat?"

"Don't call little Henry a brat!"

"Is he the father?" Nephi roared.

"Dad, I wouldn't marry that lazy trash if he was the last man in the world."

"He's a man, ain't he? He's a husband, ain't he? He's got a name, ain't he? That brat needs a name!"

"I won't marry him!" Anita declared.

"That's what you think," Nephi said. "All right, men, gimme that lad off'n that pole. He's mine!"

"What are you waiting for, men?" Jackson demanded. "Let's get going!" As between the frying pan and the fire, the choice was simple.

"You shut up, sprout!" Nephi ordered. "You're not sneaking out of this valley on no rail!"

"I demand my rights," Jackson said. "I got my mind all made up for it now."

"He can get married afterwards," Reed Carter said.

"Got something there, Reed," Young Merrill admitted. "Don't sees how one has to interfere with the other."

"The hell you say!" Nephi cried. "I don't want him maybe crippled up for the wedding. And anyhow it ain't dignified. What do you want to do, disgrace a man on the eve of his marriage?"

"Put him down, men," Young Merrill said. Jackson again had his feet on the ground.

Nephi grabbed him by the collar, twisting the parachute-silk muffler. "Jack, I don't intend to stand guard over you tonight. I'm going to treat you like a man and put you on your honor. And I got too much to do anyhow. So you *be* here when I get back with the license from Tooele. You're on your honor, and if you try to skip out I'll hunt you down and shoot you like a dog. Understand?"

Jackson nodded. The cinch on his neck made it impossible to speak.

Nephi grabbed his daughter and took her away. The mob dispersed, somewhat embarrassed. Jackson took off at a fast clip across the brush.

CHAPTER EIGHTEEN

Even the merciful oblivion of sleep was denied him. He tossed and turned through the night. He'd solved the problem of the broken bed by simply tossing the head- and footboards into a corner; something was the matter with what remained, and he had to curl unnaturally to avoid large and hard knobs under the thin mattress. Once, in the night, he fancied the kitchen door screaked open and cautious footsteps sounded in the house. Had the mob, thinking it over, come to get him again? Had Nephi changed his mind about leaving him on his honor? But, listening, breathless, he finally decided it was imagination. Or the mice. As dawn came he fell asleep finally, and was almost immediately awakened by a hammering at the door. He decided to ignore it. He didn't want to see anybody. Now or ever.

"Jack! Hey, Jack!" Ned Holt's face was at the bedroom window. "Hey, Jack! Wake up!"

"Go away. Go a long ways away."

"I got to see you, Jack."

"You're looking at me. What the hell do you want?"

"Jack, you can't lay there in bed. It's daylight. You got a big day ahead."

"You're telling me." Jackson got up, pulled on his pants, and met the sheepherder in the kitchen.

"You better fix breakfast while we talk," Ned Holt suggested. "I ain't et yet either."

Jackson began making a fire. "What'll you have, eggs or hot cakes?"

"Both. Jack, I want you to understand the whole thing. I'm sorry about last night. I didn't know. You can see how it looked to me."

"Forget it."

"Jack, Beulah's the only girl I ever wanted in my life. I'm older'n she is. I was earning a man's wages when she was born. And a funny thing. She was the cutest baby I ever seen in my born life and she growed up pretty as a picture. And I got the idea way back I don't know when that she was going to grow up and be my wife. That's crazy, but it's the way it is. And that's why I done what I done."

"It's over with, now." Jackson put on the coffee pot.

"I don't mean last night, Jack. What I done was for a nest egg for Beulah and me. No coffee for me."

"It's Coffee-Near," Jackson said bitterly. "Just wholesome grains and fruits and berries. What did you do?"

"Well, I'll try a cup. Never mind what I done, but it was something I shouldn't of. A sheepherder don't cut much ice with a girl. I wanted to get ahead. Jack, I ain't never wasted much love on you. About the time Beulah was old enough, you was there."

"Why don't you save it, Ned?"

"But I got to tell you this. And then last night after the fracas I asked Beulah to marry me and she said first she'd have to tell me. So she told me how it happened last night. And so then I had to tell her about me and what I'd done. And she said she didn't want no part of no money got that way, so I better give it back. We want to start off fresh. And your granddad was down here talking to Milo and you, and things like that make a man think. I never did like what I done. I just got started and one thing led to another. I and Beulah, we figure on going through the Temple after I've worked up and lived good enough for a recommend. And I couldn't do that without trying to make things right and—here, Jack."

Ned Holt drew a wad of bills from his pocket and set them on the backless chair.

"What's that?" Jackson said.

"It's my share for what I done. I always kept it separate. Never spent a dime of it. Take it, Jack."

"Why give it to me?"

"Jack, you never would of said what you did about settling the Trouble, except your granddad he told you to. I and Beulah, we figure it's a sign. You don't know how good I feel, Jack, getting shuck of it. You don't know how it's been a-festering. Use it for a start in building the church in the valley here. It's the only way you can clean that kind of money."

Jackson went into the other room and, rummaging among a pile of trash, found an old notebook. He went back to the kitchen and got a pencil. "O.K., I'll put it down. Donations. Ned Holt—how much?"

"Jack, you can't tell nobody where it come from. Me, I'm not supposed to have that kind of money to be donating. I'm only a sheepherder."

"I'm only lazy trash and everybody knows I'm broke. Money don't grow on bushes. Where'll I say *I* got it?"

"Just say you found it. Old house like this, you might find anything. Everybody says your granddad Skinner was well fixed, but your ma and pa never had nothing. Folks wonder if he tucked some away somewheres."

"He didn't have as much as folks thought, and my folks went through what he did have. And anyhow, them bills of yours has got dates on 'em."

"Well, Jack, I don't give a damn what you say about it. But I'm shuck of that money." The sheepherder sighed. "Sure good to get rid of that money."

"You can go shuck it onto somebody else," Jackson declared. "You're not palming it off on me. What would happen, me popping up with cash of that color? How much is it?"

"Jack, you ain't showing the right spirit. Here I come here with my heart overflowing with sacrifice, and you throw it back in my face. That ain't right."

"How much is it?"

"Well, it's twenty-eight hundred and sixty dollars. Ain't so much, figuring his cut . . ."

"Whose cut?"

"All these years, too. That's what Beulah said. She said she couldn't start life out together with me under a cloud when it was only twenty-eight hundred and sixty dollars for all them years of sin. Ain't worth it, she said. Figure it up on a yearly basis, she said. Guess I been a chump, all right. But I figured at the time it was velvet. He must of made a fortune."

"Who?"

"Jack, I can't tell you everything. I got a future to think about. Just take the money for building the meetinghouse."

"Not on your life. I'm in enough trouble now, without flashing money I can't explain. What about the income tax people?"

"But I'm trying to make up for my past sins. I want to give it for building the church."

"Go and give it to the bishop."

"I don't want him to know, or how'll I *ever* get a recommend?"

"It's your baby. Don't try to work me into it."

Ned glumly put the money in his pocket. Jackson began stirring up batter for buckwheat cakes. "None for me, Jack," Ned said. "Guess I ain't hungry." He indicated the coffee pot. "Just a cup of that stuff for me. What'll Beulah say? I got to get rid of this. I felt so good, coming here to donate it to the new meetinghouse."

With the coffee done, Ned took a cup and sipped of it critically. "Coffee-Near, you say?"

"Just an old family recipe we got from the Indians," Jackson said.

Ned took another sip, brooding. Then his eyes came up and his jaw set. "Jack, I owe you something. I done you plenty dirt."

"Me? We always got along, Ned."

"That's the worst of it. You don't know. I always told myself if I didn't do it for him, somebody else would. But still I done it, and I ought to square myself somehow. Especially since you won't take the money." Ned drew a worn billfold from his pocket and extracted a piece of paper, gray, and worn at the creases.

"Jack, I like my coffee. I know it's wrong, but I do. We had an old Indian recipe in our family, too. But those old Indian recipes ain't no good. They all use barley. So out in the sheep camp I been trying around one thing and another. Must of kept at it eight, nine year, a'fore I got it right. I figured maybe sometime I'd make it up and peddle it around to people who want a good wholesome drink. Here, Jack; I want you to have it. It'll pay back what I done to you."

"Well, if it'll make you feel better," Jackson said, taking the paper. He unfolded it, and saw the entire page filled with ingredients and directions. He'd tasted these weird concoctions before. "Thanks, Ned. I sure appreciate this."

"You'll never drink this stuff again, once you taste that."

Jackson tried to act pleased. "Sure good of you."

"Good morning," a voice said. Ned started, spilling coffee onto his legs. The bishop's face was at the hole in the door.

"Come in, Bishop," Jackson invited. The bishop did so, sniffing the aroma with anticipation.

"Er—I'm just going," Ned Holt said nervously. "Jack— about that matter—er—if it got out . . ."

"I won't say nothing."

"Don't let me run you off," the bishop said.

"Just going anyhow, Bishop." Ned gulped his coffee, grabbed his throat as the scalding stuff went down, and left.

The bishop sat on the box Ned had vacated. "Seemed in a rush."

"Coffee-Near, Bishop?"

"Don't care if I do. My! That smells wonderful!"

"Any—er—harmful effects?" Jackson asked delicately.

"Why should there be? Wholesome grains and berries. None of the harmful affects of coffee. I took a cup last night just before bedtime. Ah, delicious!"

"And slept like a baby?" Jackson asked hopefully.

"I had a lot on my mind to keep me awake." The bishop accepted a cup and inhaled the fragrance. "Ah! Haven't changed your mind about doing a little business?"

"Can't see my way clear."

"How do you feel this morning? All ready to get married?"

"No; I'm not."

"That's no attitude, Jackson. Nephi and Anita left for Tooele an hour or so ago after the license. Won't make much time in that Model T, but it's reliable; they'll be back this afternoon. And I'll perform the ceremony. I'm glad to have the mess cleared up. Though it couldn't be at a worse time for me. Now I won't be able to start for Salt Lake until after the ceremony, and I hate night driving. Of course Sister Jensen will go with Henry and Katie. They ought to be on their way by now." The bishop looked into his coffee cup. "I just thought you might have a few words to tell me privately."

"I sure have."

"Fine, Jackson. Clear the air, I always say."

"The whole thing's a frame-up. I was never so much as out with Anita in my life. I don't have nothing to do with that brat of hers."

"That's no attitude, Jackson. Face it like a man."

"But how am I going to marry Katie if I'm railroaded into this?"

"Jackson, after a thing like this you can never marry Katie. She's on her way right now with Henry and Sister Jensen to Salt Lake. The Lord moves in a mysterious way."

"Et yet?"

"I've been so busy, Katie getting ready and all—"

"Eggs or buckwheat cakes?"

"I'll take an egg on the cakes."

Jackson finished stirring the batter. He greased the top of the stove with a bacon rind, poured six circles of batter, and broke four eggs.

"Henry wonders if you could help out at the store," the bishop said. "Milo's getting old. And he skedaddled last night. Just up and went somewhere with Henry's weapons carrier. Henry all fixed to leave this morning, too. It doesn't show much consideration. Henry says it's a steady job for you. A man getting married has to think about that."

"I don't want nothing out of Henry Brown."

"He's just helping you out. Take the job anyhow until he gets back from the honeymoon. Matter of fact, I suggested it. He was going to have Ned Holt take over the store while he was away. Of course Milo ought to be back, but nobody knows where he went."

"What about *my* honeymoon?"

The bishop cleared his throat. "Under the circumstances, Jackson . . ."

"I mean my honeymoon with Katie."

"Jackson, I feel that somewhere there's a mistake in that matter."

"Grandpa Skinner was plain enough. And you said yourself you'd heard a voice saying it was all right if I settled the Trouble."

"Jackson, we must hold faith. Very often these messages are symbolical. Maybe Katie will be your wife in spirit sometime. I don't know." The bishop sighed. "I hear Apostle Black is very low. We must hold faith." The bishop, truth to tell, was having a harder inward struggle than he cared to admit. For the first time in his life he'd heard a voice from beyond. And things weren't panning out at all as they should have done. Instead of settling the Trouble, Jackson had merely picked off the scab.

Jackson dished up the hot cakes and eggs. He got the syrup can from the shelf, setting aside a bricklike package atop the can, opened the can, poured syrup over the hot cakes and eggs, put the can back on the shelf, and then picked up the bricklike package curiously. It was wrapped in brown paper, tied with twine, and the whole thing had been dipped in hot wax.

"What have you got there?" the biship asked.

"First time I ever seen it."

"Maybe something of your father's."

"The house is in a mess, but I sure know what's on that shelf." Jackson got out his pocket knife, cut the string, slit the wax along the seams of the paper, unwrapped the paper, and exposed a thick packet of currency. "Well, look at that."

"I declare," the bishop declared.

Jackson leafed through the currency. "All hundreds. Gold certificates."

"I do declare."

Jackson wet a thumb and began counting. Finished, he raised bleak eyes.

"How much?"

Jackson swallowed. "Two hundred and fifty of 'em."

"That's—let's see—that's twenty-five thousand dollars."

"That's a lot of money," Jackson said. "We'd better eat the hot cakes before they get cold."

CHAPTER NINETEEN

Jackson put the currency on the floor and began to eat. The bishop kept glancing at the money as he ate.

"What I can't figure," Jackson said finally, "is how it got there. It wasn't there yesterday."

"You never saw it before?"

"Sure I never saw it before."

"Just sitting there on top of the syrup can all of a sudden."

"That's right." Jackson waved his fork angrily. "And it's going too far! They can't do this to me! First Ned Holt wants to give me money, and now this!"

"Ned Holt? Why?"

"He didn't say. And there's no note on this package, neither. It ain't that I hate money. I wish I had twenty-five thousand dollars. But these days you better not pop up suddenly with dough like that, or the old guy with the whiskers will put you away."

"Certainly puts you on the spot," the bishop said dryly.

"I wonder." Jackson cocked an eye at the green-canvas ceiling. "Last night I thought maybe I heard somebody come in. Then I thought it must be the mice. But now I guess it must of been somebody. Somebody come in here and left this and snuck out. Well, it's lucky you was here, Bishop. You know I didn't know what was in that package before I unwrapped it."

"I know what you *said*," the bishop amended quietly.

"Bishop, you know very well I didn't have no twenty-five thousand dollars yesterday."

"I know you shouldn't have had twenty-five cents. That's what makes it so peculiar. Jackson, I am not a baby. Nobody in the world is going to creep in here and plant a fortune on you."

"Bishop, you was sitting right there when—"

"Let's understand one another, Jackson. I think it's mighty convenient of you to have the bishop as witness. But all I know is what happened. I was watching you. You took that package off the can, opened the can and poured the syrup, put the lid on the can, and put the can on the shelf. Then you picked up the package and acted surprised. Why didn't you open the package in the first place? Afraid the hot cakes would get cold?"

"I wasn't paying attention. It took a while to sink in. Well, I don't care whether you believe it or not. Somebody planted this on me, and I'm going to find out who or know the reason why. Ready?"

"Aren't you going to finish eating?"

"Appetite's gone."

The bishop shook his head with slow wonder. Assuming the boy's story was true—with all else Jackson had on his head, it took a present of twenty-five thousand dollars to upset his appetite.

"I suppose Henry and Katie are halfway to Wendover by

now," the bishop said as he drove toward the store. "A fine couple, good match. Popular. Everybody likes them. You should have seen the crowd on hand to say good-bye. And so early in the morning, too; just breaking dawn. Of course the dance had just let out, but it shows their spirit was in the right place. I hope Nephi gets back in good shape this afternoon. I hate to drive at night. That old Model T's slow."

"Good of you to stay on my account," Jackson said, feeling some comment was necessary.

"What are you going to do with the money?"

"I'm going to find the sneak who palmed it off on me if it's the last thing I do. I got enough to worry about."

"You're a strange one, Jackson. One thing about you, once you've got a story you stick to it. What's that?" The bishop peered ahead as he rounded Henry's stack yards. "Is that Henry's car, still there?"

"It sure is," Jackson said, feeling suddenly happy.

"Oh, my goodness, I hope nothing happened."

A group of men, shivering in the chill morning, were talking together by the store. "Where's Henry?" the bishop asked.

"Henry?" Young Merrill Littlewall said. "Why, he's in the house, Bishop. And I reckon he'll stay there awhile."

The bishop hurried into the house.

"What's up?" Jackson asked. "What happened?"

The men ignored him.

"All right, be snooty. I don't want no more to do with you than you do with me. But I got something to say."

"Keep it to yourself," Reed Carter advised.

"Can't you take a hint?" Young Merrill Littlewall said.

Sid Worth said, "Go off somewheres and talk to yourself!" Sid was highly infuriated with Jackson. A bachelor, Sid had left the dance early with a girl. He'd got no place with the girl, and while he was gone the big fracas had occurred. Sid dearly loved to be in the middle of things, and he was furious that Jackson should have got himself into a ruckus while he was gone.

Jackson unwrapped the brick of currency. "I just want to say this. I got twenty-five thousand dollars here. Found it in my house this morning."

The aloofness of the men melted like snow on the desert's dusty face. They were all attention. "Found it?" Young Merrill Littlewall said. "Found it, you say, Jack?"

"On top of my syrup can on the kitchen shelf." Jackson ran a thumb along the edge of the currency. "All hundreds. The old-style bills. Gold certificates."

"Let me see," Reed Carter said.

"No, you don't. Nobody gets a close look at these bills to memorize a couple of serial numbers or notice some mark on one of 'em. I guess the man who put 'em there will be able to tell me enough when he claims 'em."

"Put 'em there?" Sid Worth asked.

"Some sneak snuck in last night and planted this money on me."

The men exchanged glances. Sid said, "Just crept in and left all that money there and run like hell. Twenty-five thousand, huh?"

"That's right."

"Just slipped it there on the shelf while you was asleep. Valley ain't what it used to be. In the old days nobody locked a door. Now you don't trust nobody. Liable to creep in and leave a fortune while a man's helpless and can't defend himself."

"An outrage," Young Merrill Littlewall admitted.

"To think somebody in the valley would do a thing like that," Reed Carter said. "Maybe somebody we've knowed and trusted all our lives."

"What's the matter with you guys?" Jackson demanded. "Can't you believe the simple truth? You know I don't own this kind of money."

"Them's gold certificates," Young Merrill said. "You should of turned 'em in years ago, Jack."

"How could I, you knotheads! It wasn't there before this morning!"

"Hear you're fixing your place up some," Reed Carter observed casually.

"Wouldn't be tearing off that old canvas lining, getting the house in shape for the new wife?" Young Merrill said.

"This here money wasn't hidden between the walls!" Jackson yelled. "I'm telling you how it happened! Somebody planted it on me! And anyhow if it was hid in the house the mice would of chewed it up for nests years ago."

"That's right," Sid Worth agreed. "Especially since nobody would ever think of putting it inside a tin can."

"Always figured old Moroni Skinner must of stashed some away somewheres," Young Merrill said.

"Didn't take you long to find it after he appeared," Reed Carter pointed out.

"Oh, go to hell, the pack of you," Jackson snapped. "I'll get Henry to keep it in the store safe. Whoever planted it on me can come ask for it and no questions. And if he shows up pretty soon, I won't make trouble for him."

"Serious business," Sid Worth agreed, "planting a fortune on a man. Sure glad nobody pulls dirty tricks like that on me."

Jackson turned away, partly from frustration and partly because he saw Katie behind Henry's house, drifting toward the line of willows along the creek in the back yard. Jackson found her at the little patio behind the willows. Milo Ferguson had fixed the place years ago for his wife. Henry, an active man with little use for invitations to sit and relax, had let it go to pot. The lily pond was dry and weeds had grown up between the paving stones. Katie was sitting on the rustic bench; she was all dressed up for travel, and cute as a button.

"Why don't you go off somewhere and die?" she greeted. "A long ways off and stay there?"

"What's wrong now, darling?"

"One more pet word and I'll bop you with this bench, so help me."

He squatted on his heels by the lily pond and his hand felt unconsciously for tobacco in his shirt pocket. He drew the hand away. "You've got me wrong. Wait and see. It'll all work out somehow."

"You're a blight. You're like the plague. You just walk by and people never recover. You were disgusting last night."

"You don't understand—"

"Let it ride, will you? And if it wasn't for you I'd be on my way right now to Salt Lake."

"You can't blame me for that, whatever it is."

"Oh, I can't blame you for that! In the first place, if it wasn't for last night, Dad wouldn't have had to stay behind to marry you and Anita. You had nothing to do with that, did you?"

"No, I didn't. And you'll find out sometime."

"Then Milo disappeared."

"Hell, I'm not Milo's keeper."

"It's something to do with you; I'm sure of it. And I guess you had nothing to do with that disgusting business with Beulah Hess last night, either?"

Jackson was silent. After all, a girl's good name . . .

"Oh, I know you never attacked her!" Katie cried furiously.

"What? You know I didn't?" Jackson beamed.

"Don't squat there grinning like a Chessie cat. It would have been much better if you *had*."

"I don't think you feel well," Jackson said, puzzled.

"I feel fine. I feel wonderful. How do you think I feel, you fool? All ready to go. Mother in the back seat. Shaking hands. Saying good-bye. Somebody tying tin cans to the back of the car. Corny jokes. Henry started the motor and put the car in gear. And then Beulah's father came storming in. Why, sure, I feel swell! I never was so humiliated in my born life!"

"Where do I come in?"

"That's a question. That's good. Where do you come in! What do you suppose made Ross Hess wild, anyhow? You know what a temper he's got. When Beulah got home from the dance her father was going to kill you for attacking her. Ross Hess goes crazy when he's mad. So she broke down and said Henry put her up to it."

"Well, that makes it my fault."

"It's only natural that Henry should do something, the way you acted. You and Milo tricking him with a trumped-up story of a visitation. Henry was just fighting back the best way he could, poor dear."

"Did Ross hurt him bad?"

"It's his back. He's got that trick sacroiliac. Another minute and we'd be gone. Then Ross Hess drove up roaring mad. It was horrible. Poor Henry trying to keep him off. And then they fell down in the dust, and Henry in his new suit and all. And then Henry was suddenly still and white, and Ross got off him. It scared Ross. Henry just lying there quietly. And nobody could help him. It must be terrible to have a trick back. And now it's three weeks. Two, anyhow. It would kill him to ride in a car. And I don't thank you for any part of this, Jack Whitetop!"

Two weeks! Jackson felt that anything could happen in two weeks. If yesterday was any criterion, a lot would. Come to think about it, if Beulah Hess hadn't made the fuss last night, Henry and Katie would right now be a good leg on the way to Salt Lake. Certainly was remarkable how things were working out.

"And don't sit there grinning!" Katie said. "Don't forget you're getting married this afternoon!"

"Why remind me of that when I'm happy?"

"Jack, I never was so mortified. A fellow like you mixed up in such a mess. Yesterday—well, it was crazy, you talking about cutting Henry out and all. But it was exciting and sort of thrilling in a way. I knew it couldn't ever be, but still—. You're a handsome devil, you know, even though utterly worthless. And then to find you mixed up in a mess like that."

"Oh, so that's why you're sore," Jackson said.

"Good heavens. You don't suppose I'm interested in *you?* I couldn't care less. It's when you mess up my own affairs that it matters."

"I don't think Anita was herself last night."

"What girl would be, seeing the father of her child on a rail? She's got spunk, I'll hand that to her. If you were heel enough not to give the child a name, she wouldn't beg you."

"I was overseas when the brat was born."

"Get somebody to tell you about the birds and the bees sometime. She had the baby six months after you'd sailed. And to think you came back here, Jack, on your furlough before going overseas. You came back here and stepped out with me. You know, that's a rotten thing to do. You might have spent the time with her. No wonder she doesn't want you."

"Katie!" her father's voice called.

"Right here, Dad!"

The bishop was on the rear porch. "I guess we'd better go home. There's nothing we can do now but wait. He's all right except when he tries to move."

"Dad, we ought to get a doctor."

"You know how he feels about that. He says a doctor would put him in a plaster cast for six weeks, and if he just lets Nature take its course he'll get better by himself in three. I'll have the elders in this afternoon. We just have to wait it out."

They went out to the bishop's car. The crowd had

dispersed, having chewed the juice out of events. Sister Jensen glared at Jackson from the rear seat. A streamer of dust was coming; the bishop waited. Ross Hess drove in. His temper gone, the little man had a hang-dog contriteness. He was always dreadfully sorry after an outbreak. An old Indian was beside him in the front seat.

"I went up to the reservation and got Charlie Littleface here," Ross Hess said. "I'm sorry about what happened. They say Charlie Littleface is good with things like that."

"What can you do, Charlie?" the bishop asked.

"Two dollar," the Indian said.

"Cheap enough," Ross Hess said. "They say he's wonderful."

"I'm going to have the elders in."

"Charlie's a bonesetter. What can we lose at two dollars?"

"Did you tell him what it was?"

"Yes."

"Can you fix it, Charlie?"

The Indian nodded. "Two dollar."

"We're not getting any place," the bishop said. "Let's go in and see."

Henry was in his east bedroom lying on a piece of plywood set over the bed. Ross Hess said, "Henry, Charlie Littleface here is a bonesetter. Maybe he can help you."

"Don't touch me!" Henry yelled.

The Indian surveyed Henry impassively. He put his hand on his own back at the juncture of shirt and sagging pants. "Huh?"

"You know what it is, pal," Henry admitted.

Charlie Littleface squatted on his heels and rolled a cigarette. He smoked it slowly and deliberately, then arose.
"Two dollar," he said after having thought it over.

"You'll get your money," the bishop said.

With a flip of the hand the Indian motioned Henry to
turn over. "All right, but keep your hands off me!" Henry
cried. "You, too!" he screamed, as Katie tried to help him.
It was painful, watching Henry turn over. He moved with
a terrible exquisite delicacy, conscious of the play of every
muscle, freezing occasionally. It took him two full minutes
to turn over. He carefully relaxed on his stomach, gasping,
with sweat beaded on his face.

"If you hurt me I'll kill you," he said.

The Indian began probing gently at Henry's spine, not
down where it hurt, but above it, up the spine and to the
neck and shoulders.

"He's a phony," Henry said. "Look, Charlie, it hurts
lower down. But go easy."

The Indian kept working on the upper spine, fingers
clawing at nerve centers. It was almost an hour later when
with a flip of the hand he motioned Henry to turn onto
his back. This time Henry turned carefully but easily. The
Indian brought Henry's legs up one at a time, bent them at
the knees, twisted slightly, bore down, and there was a tiny
click. Charlie Littleface squatted on his heels and rolled
another cigarette. He smoked it to the stub, dropped the
stub on the carpet, and arose.

"Two dollar."

"You mean that's all?" Henry said. "You didn't do
nothing."

"Two dollar."

"O.K. He's a phony but he didn't do any harm. I'll pay him." Henry raised onto an elbow and felt in a pocket. Then he realized what he'd done. Carefully, he got to a sitting position. Then he got off the bed. "Well, I'll be doggoned!" he cried. "Charlie, you're wonderful! It's gone! I'm all right! What did you do?"

"Two dollar," Charlie Littleface said.

Henry paid him.

"I'm glad you're all right, Henry," Ross Hess said. "I feel terrible about what happened."

"Travel?" the bishop asked Charlie Littleface, making motions of steering a car. "Him O.K.? Ride automobile? bump, bump, bump, O.K. Charlie?"

"He's all right," the Indian said, his palm and tongue having, apparently, some connection. "Good as new. Let's go, Ross." He and Ross went out.

"These Indians," Sister Jensen said. "Why, he can talk as good as I can." She beamed. "I'm certainly glad you're all right, Henry. I'm thankful I don't have to waste this hairdo. Sister Ormand almost talked a leg off me while she was fixing it."

"You can still make good time, Henry," the bishop said. "It's early yet."

"Henry, are you sure you're all right?" Katie said dubiously.

Henry was bending, twisting, feeling. "I'm as good as new, and only two dollars. I'd give a hundred any time. You don't know what hell it is. Why didn't somebody tell me about Charlie Littleface before?"

"There's some heathen trick to it," Sister Jensen said darkly.

"Now, Ma," the bishop reproved. "Don't talk that way about our Lamanite brethren. Time's a wasting . . . Jackson, you'll tend the store while they're away."

Jackson felt that something had to be done and in a hurry. "Well, I—I guess I'll be pretty busy," he said.

"Doing what?"

"Well, Dad, that's his business," Katie said. "And, anyhow, I don't think Henry's as well as he thinks he is."

"Everything's arranged, dear," her mother said. "Hotel reservations and everything."

"I guess Henry knows how he feels," the bishop pointed out.

"I'm fit as a fiddle," Henry declared.

"But what if—" Katie said, "—your back went out in the middle of the desert or something?"

"You don't seem to be too anxious," Jackson observed.

It was the wrong thing to say. "Of course I'm anxious! I'm ready to go right now! Henry, if you really feel all right, let's go!"

"Good!" Henry cried. "Jack, it's a steady job at the store, and you'll need that."

"But I—I got to find out who belongs to this," Jackson said, dragging the brick of currency from a hind pocket. It was an inane thing to do, but it was an excuse of sorts and he certainly wasn't going to expedite Henry's marriage in any way.

"You go ahead, Henry," the bishop said, nettled. "I'll see Ned Holt about tending the store. Should have done it in the first place. You go ahead."

Henry wasn't listening. He was staring at the money. "Where did you get that?" His voice was flat.

"Somebody planted it in my house. I was making hot cakes, and I got the syrup—"

"Jackson," the bishop said, "please don't start that again. If you're going to tend the store, say so, and if you're not—"

"Let me talk to him, Bishop," Henry said in that curiously flat voice. He led Jackson to the kitchen, close the door, and indicated a chair. "Sit down." Jackson sat down. Henry walked back and forth a number of times. Then he sat down, putting a hand to his back as he eased into the chair. "O.K., Jack. What's the deal?"

"Deal?" Jackson was all innocence. "I just want to find out who belongs to this money."

"You don't know."

"I'd sure like to. I'm in enough trouble without this. It wasn't there yesterday."

"You're a smooth one," Henry said. "How did you get wise?"

"The bishop was down and I was cooking buckwheat cakes. I got the syrup can and there it was on top the can."

"O.K., play dumb!" Henry got up and paced again. "Well, what's your proposition?"

"Well, I figure to find out who belongs to it. Is it yours?"

Henry paused, smiling thinly. "It's not that easy, Jack. I'm admitting nothing. Nothing at all."

"People trying to force money onto me," Jackson complained. "First Ned Holt, and then this—"

"Ned Holt! Ned saw you?"

"Early this morning. Woke me up. Trying to give me money."

"Damn his dirty hide!" Henry said. Then he studied Jackson's face closely. "But you got this before that. You didn't have a chance afterwards."

"Huh? It was in the night. I thought I heard somebody come in at night."

"What do you want?"

"I want to find the man who owns this money."

"Playful, huh? Don't shove me too far." Henry opened the door and strode into the bedroom where Katie and her parents were waiting. "My back's hurting a little again," he said. "I think we'd better wait. A day or two anyhow."

"Oh, goodness," Sister Jensen said. "And all the reservations made."

"You know how you feel, Henry," the bishop said.

Katie confronted Jackson, and cried, "It's you! I know it's you! It's always you! He was all right before he talked with you!"

CHAPTER
TWENTY

Alone, Henry Brown bolted the doors and drew the shades. He pushed back the heavy table from the center of the living room and threw back the rug. The floor was of planking, originally held with wooden dowels which, in places, had been replaced with heavy screws. With a screwdriver he gave two of the screws a half twist, put the tool between a crack, and with a lifting pry swung a hinged section of planking open, revealing the lid of a steel strongbox imbedded in concrete below. With his own hands, behind locked doors and drawn shades, Henry Brown had fixed this place for his valuables. A tough job, too, because he was all fingers and thumbs with tools. But he'd trusted nobody with the job. He would have bet his life that nobody else knew about it. And tied around his neck by a rawhide thong was the one and only key. The lock couldn't be picked.

The box showed no signs of having been tampered with, and as he unlocked it he wondered if he'd been wrong. Of course nobody could get into this strongbox, even if its whereabouts were known. His hidden cache was a source of great satisfaction to Henry Brown. It was tangible evidence that he was a very smart hombre. It stood as a symbol of his resentment against the outrage of meddling government controls and the income tax, which penalized a man of industry and initiative, unless he was smart enough to get around things.

His one worry about the approaching marriage to Katie had been the key. He couldn't hide the existence of the key, what with sharing the marriage bed. He'd been reluctant to hide it somewhere. There was always the possibility of somebody stumbling onto it. And he liked the feel of it around his neck as a comfortable reminder. He'd thought that at first he'd make a joke of the key. Say it was a good luck charm or something. And then he'd lead up to it, and eventually, tell her. Be best after all if two people knew. Katie was a bright girl. She certainly, if properly prepared, would see the thing in the right light.

He raised the steel lid. Inside was a tin box, beside it a small sack of calcium chloride to absorb any vagrant trace of moisture, and beside the sack were two bricklike packages in brown paper tied with string, and dipped in melted wax.

Yesterday afternoon there had been three packages.

Henry opened the tin box and counted eighty-seven hundred dollars in hundred-dollar bills. Nothing was missing except the one packet, containing twenty-five thousand dollars. If robbery, why wasn't it all gone?

He studied the lid and the lock of the strongbox again. The lid hadn't been forced. The pin-tumbler lock couldn't be picked, and there was no sign of tampering.

It was impossible. Except the one packet was gone and he'd seen it with his own eyes in Jackson's hands.

And now Jackson had the brassbound gall to flaunt the money in Henry's face and dare him to claim it!

"That crook! That miserable sneak thief!" Henry cried.

Then, suddenly breathless, he looked cautiously about the gloom of the room as if unseen eyes were watching through the walls or the drawn shades. Nobody could know of this cache, unless—His stomach tightened with the pagan's superstitious terror of the unknown. His duplicity, his hypocrisy—this visitation business of the Saints—spirits appearing from beyond with messages—Sister Ormand stuff. Was there something in it? Even Milo had claimed to have had a visitation yesterday. An apostate. Jackson Whitetop, a shiftless ne'er-do-well like his father before him, suddenly had announced that he'd marry Katie. One thing after another had happened since then. Henry had had a quarrel with Katie and she'd ridden to the store in Jackson's buckboard. Jackson had taken her to the dance. Henry had put a bug in Beulah's ear and that had backfired; because of that Henry had thrown his back out instead of taking Katie to Salt Lake. And then Jackson had flashed the money, when Henry was on the verge of going again.

True, Jackson would have to marry Anita. But would he? Would something again turn up? What, Henry wondered, was he up against? How else could Jackson have got that money, except through the fiendish help of spirits? Were beings—unseen eyes—watching him this very second? If the secret strongbox wasn't safe, what would be?

Henry felt helpless in the grip of an implacable fate. His luck had turned. Everything was going bad. But he wouldn't go down without a fight. There was always a way with a man who wouldn't give up.

The bishop had driven off in too big a huff to remember that Jackson had no means of transportation. Jackson didn't contemplate the prospect of a two-mile hike with relish. Army basics had confirmed a rancher's deep aversion to walking, and anyhow he was wearing riding boots which weren't made for it. He hung around the store awhile, but nobody showed up. The mail wasn't due for hours, and people were home sleeping the sleep of the just after the dance. He improved his time with a stub pencil and a scrap of paper, printing a little notice which he impaled on a splinter of a porch post:

FOUND

$25,000

Owner Please Apply to Jackson Whitetop

and Collect

The prospect of a ride seemed remote. Jackson considered the matter at some length and then reluctantly began walking down the dusty road. By the time he'd walked a half-mile his feet were hurting and he sat down to consider things. The domestication of the horse was without doubt the thing that had raised the human race above the animals. A streamer of dust appeared from the south and he waited hopefully. Katie drove up.

"Dad forgot you'd have to walk, until we'd got home awhile."

He got in and relaxed thankfully. "Whew."

"You act like you're half killed. What would happen if you did a day's work?"

"I hate to think," he admitted.

"Jack, you'd ought to be ashamed of yourself."

"I am," he agreed. "I could of borrowed a horse from Henry. Should of. Even if he didn't seem in a good mood."

"Why can't you ever talk sense?"

"You mean Anita? I told you I never had anything to do with her brat."

"It's this visitation business. You had no right imposing on Dad's faith with a story like that."

"Oh. He told you?"

"I knew all about it. Mother told me when we got home. She's worried about Dad. He's all mixed up. What happened this morning has made it worse. Mother doesn't know what to do. She knows you never did have any visitation from your grandfather."

"What do you think?"

"I certainly can't see why he'd appear to an apostate. And you're certainly not worthy yourself. If Milo had *had* a visitation he certainly wouldn't go around smoking those horrible cigars afterwards. Mother says you cooked up the whole thing with Milo. And if your grandfather *did* appear to you, he certainly wouldn't tell you to marry *me*. That's the silliest thing I ever heard of in my born life."

"I can think of a lot of things sillier."

"You've gone ahead and got Dad all worked up. You played on his faith. It isn't fair or sporting or ethical. If you *did* have a visitation you could have kept it to yourself."

"I didn't talk about it. It just got around. Milo shot off his face."

"Very clever, too. You remaining silent while Milo spreads the word. It's impressive, coming from an apostate. Jack, I want you to do the right thing."

"I'm trying to, but things keep gumming it up. I feel like somebody caught in a machine."

"I want you to go to Dad and tell him you cooked the whole thing up."

Jackson considered. She evidently didn't know that her father had heard a voice, himself. "I couldn't do that. It wouldn't be true."

"Jack, what do you think of me?"

"Honey, ever since I was knee high to—"

"See?" she broke in. "You claim you like me, and yet you do this to Dad. I'm terribly humiliated, Jack. I'm supposed to be on my way right now to Salt Lake to get married. And it's all your fault I'm not. Haven't you got any mercy? Won't you go to Dad, for my sake?"

"You're not making it easy for me."

"What difference would it make, anyhow? If you *did* have a visitation, nothing you can say will change it. And Dad will be relieved. He's all sixes and sevens."

He didn't answer, and she cried, "Can't you see how impossible the whole thing is? You'll be married to Anita this afternoon anyhow. You could at least relieve Dad's worries."

He said nothing.

"All right, go to hell," she snapped. She turned into his lane. "Poor Anita. No wonder she didn't want to marry you. What can you do with a wife? How can you support her? Do you expect her to live in that dump?"

"That's a good house, fundamentally."

"And you're a good man, fundamentally. But neither you or the house will ever amount to a hill of beans."

"Built solid. Don't make 'em that way no more. Solid pine logs with cedar underpinnings. All it needs is a little fixing up."

"And just who's going to come along to do it for you? Maybe your Grandpa Skinner will send some angels down to fix it up. Quietly, of course, so as not to disturb your rest."

Jackson sighed. Katie was sure ornery this morning. But cute as a button. Yep, cute as a bug's ear.

She slammed on the brakes, and Reed Carter rose into view from behind the woodpile. "Hello, Jack. Been waiting for you."

"Walk?" Jackson looked around for Reed's car.

"Nothing like a little hike in the morning, Jack."

The kitchen door opened and the iron-gray hair of Young Merrill Littlewall came into view. "Well," he said to Reed Carter, "what you sneaking around here for?"

"How'd *you* git here?"

"I was here first. A man's got a right to take a horseback ride, ain't he?"

"On what?"

"Come up the back way and left the horse in the willows. Cooler down there. I always take care of my horseflesh."

Reed Carter squinted at the rim of the sun rising on the chill valley. "Considerate. It might get sunburned."

"I was here first . . . Jack, I want to see you."

"I'm already talking with him."

"I got here first."

"Jack's talking to me."

"Jack," Young Merrill said, "what I want to do is fix up your house for you."

"Don't you listen to him, Jack!" Reed Carter said. "*I'm* going to fix your house up!"

"It beats me," Katie murmured, shaking her head. "Jack, it beats me."

"Angels," Jackson said.

CHAPTER
TWENTY-ONE

Young Merrill strolled over to the car. "Yep, Jack, you getting married and all—you know how us valley folks are. We want to pitch in and give you a good send-off."

"Just a minute, Merrill," Reed Carter bristled. "Us north-valley folks can take care of our own affairs without no butting in by the south— Jack, don't you have no truck with them south-valley people. Let me tell you what I been figuring on for your house."

"If some people don't have the common ordinary decency to wait their turn, well, something can maybe be done about it," Young Merrill stated.

"You and who else?" Reed Carter asked.

"Wait a minute before you make a ruckus," Jackson said placatingly. "It's awful fine of both you men. In fact I'm overwhelmed." Which was putting it mildly. "But you see, I figure on doing it myself."

"Jack, you wouldn't want to do that," Young Merrill Littlewall said, injured. "You got to let me do *something* for you. Some little thing like fixing your house over real nice. You only get married once."

"Us north-valley folks always pitches in for a young couple," Reed Carter said. "You just go on your honeymoon, you and Anita. Let me take care of everything."

"I can't afford to have it done. I'll be scratching to dig up materials."

Young Merrill laughed. "Money? Why, Jack, I told you it was a wedding present!"

"That's sure swell of you, Merrill."

"Not so fast, Jack!" Reed Carter cried. "You live in the north end, sort of. Deal with me, Jack."

"Let's see if I have this straight," Katie said. There was a twinkle in her eye. "Am I to understand both of you are willing to fix his house up free of charge?"

"Certainly," Young Merrill said.

"Wedding present," Reed Carter said.

"Angels," Katie said.

"Just folks," Reed Carter said modestly.

Young Merrill gazed east across the valley. "Somebody's a-coming!"

"Must be Sid Worth," Jackson said, surveying the dust. "And sure hitting that road."

"Well, damn his hide!" Young Merrill said.

"What business *he* got butting in!" Reed Carter said.

"We ain't going to let them dry farmers mix in ranchers' affairs," Young Merrill said.

"Not on your life."

Reed Carter and Young Merrill met each other's eye in the sudden realization that they were agreeing on a common course of action. A bit sheepishly, they moved off together for a hurried consultation.

"What gives?" Jackson said.

"I think you've got another prospect," Katie said. "This is marvelous!"

"I don't get it."

"Keep right on playing dumb. I'll handle the clutches."

"Real kind of 'em, ain't it?"

"Very," Katie said.

The two ranchers shook hands and turned to the car. Young Merrill, speaking in a voice of brotherhood slightly marred by haste, as he cocked a worried eye at the rapidly approaching dust from the east said, "Jack, there's no use of us fighting about this. We both want to do it for you, so why not both of us do it? We'll pitch in and fix your place up between us, free of charge."

"Well . . ." Jackson said.

"Just what does that mean?" Katie asked. "Just what will you do to the house?"

"Do you mind if we talk to Jack alone?"

"I'm his agent."

"What?"

"She's my agent," Jackson said.

"I never heard of such an arrangement," Young Merrill said.

"Merrill, let me handle this," Reed Carter said. "Don't stand there palavering. Jack—I mean, Katie—we'll fix it up any way you want. I guarantee you'll be pleased. Is it a deal, Jack? I mean, Katie? Shake on it!"

"I think," Katie said practically, "we'd better look around inside and decide on things."

"There ain't time!"

"All the time in the world. If you're busy, Reed, maybe you can come back later."

Sid Worth's car was barreling down the lane. Reed Carter smothered an oath. Young Merrill cried, "Remember, Jack—I mean, Katie—remember that negotiations are in progress with us. Don't you go letting no dry farmers in on this!"

"Well!" Sid Worth said, pulling up. "I was watching, and the minute the car come in I started out. And you pair are already here."

"We already got the deal sewed up," Reed Carter said.

"We're fixing Jack's place up for him," Young Merrill added.

"Shook hands on it yet, Jack?" Sid asked.

"We're dealing with Katie," Young Merrill said.

"Well!" Sid exclaimed. "Don't tell me!"

"I'm just his agent in this matter," Katie said.

"Oh. Well, you shook hands on it?"

"Good-bye, Sid," Reed Carter suggested.

"What's on your mind, Sid?" Katie asked. "Figuring on fixing Jack's house as a wedding present?"

"We're going to do that now Katie," Young Merrill protested. "It's practically agreed on."

"Katie," Sid said, "you listen to my proposition before you decide. And why can't we split it up three ways? You got to give the dry farmers a break."

"Let's go inside and look it over," Katie suggested.

Young Merrill surveyed the kitchen and made a sweeping movement of the arm. "Now, take this room. What you need is new linoleum—"

"Over that old floor?" Sid asked scathingly.

Reed Carter glared at him resentfully. "Of course we'll put in a new floor. Won't we, Merrill?"

"Just in the kitchen?" Sid said.

Young Merrill glared at him resentfully. "Of course not. We'll floor the whole house."

"What kind of floors?" Sid asked nastily.

Reed and Young Merrill exchanged glances. "Pine in here and oak otherwise," the latter said.

"And we'll tear out this old green canvas," Reed Carter said. "Chink the logs and cover 'em up with wallboard."

"I think it might be nicer to leave the log wall showing," Katie said. "Don't you think so, Jack? Of course it would take a little more work. You'd have to get rid of whatever framework holds the canvas on, and put in all new chinking. The logs would be cleaned and shellacked, of course."

Reed Carter swallowed. "That's a good idea."

"And," Katie said, "what this place needs is some nice big closets."

"Closets?" Young Merrill echoed barrenly. "What for?"

"You ask a woman what she wants closets for!" Sid scoffed.

"Of course we'll put in closets," Reed Carter declared. "Who said we wouldn't?" He glared around for something to show his generosity. "And new doors and windows!"

"I think antique iron would fit the style of the house for hardware," Katie said. "The real handmade stuff. It comes a little higher, but the rest of the house will be so nice."

"Certainly," Young Merrill said doggedly. "I was going to suggest it. Well, Katie, what do you say?"

"What's your advice, agent?" Jack asked.

"Well, not so bad, Jack."

"Shake on it!" Young Merrill cried.

"Cheapskates," Sid Worth said. "What about plumbing?"

Young Merrill and Reed Carter exchanged bleak looks. "Didn't we mention plumbing?" Young Merrill asked innocently. "Of course that's included. Put a pump right here in the sink."

"Pump in the sink!" Sid sniffed. "Well, if you're done, I'll tell you what I had in mind. Windmill with a tank. Running water. Nice bathroom with automatic water heater."

"Did I say pump in the sink?" Young Merrill asked. "What I meant was it would beat even a pump in the sink. Windmill, running water, nice bathroom with automatic water heater—that's what we had in mind all along, ain't it, Reed?"

"We decided on that beforehand," Reed said. "Well, how about it?"

Jackson looked at Katie. Katie looked at Sid Worth. Sid looked innocently at the ceiling.

"Take it," Sid advised.

"Take it," Katie advised.

"Well," Jackson said. "I hardly like to impose on—"

Katie seized his hand and shoved it into the hand of Reed Carter, then that of Young Merrill, to seal the bargain.

"And now that you've made your deal," Sid Worth said, "is it my turn to negotiate?"

The two ranchers chuckled indulgently. "Go ahead, Sid!

Go ahead!"

"O.K. I'm not greedy. I'll do the finishing touches. Now, take that dirt roof. It ain't modern—"

"We mentioned shingles, didn't we?" Reed Carter blustered.

"You boys is finished," Sid said.

"That's right," Katie agreed. "It's Sid's turn."

Sid rubbed his hands together. "I'll take off that six inches of dirt on the roof and put on some nice shakes. Hand-split shakes. They go with this kind of house. And the thing you need in this country, Jack, is a good basement. A full concrete basement."

The two ranchers emitted yelps of animal pain.

"But that's too much, Sid," Jackson protested.

"Jack, shut up," Katie ordered.

"Forget it; glad to help you out," Sid said. "And there's six of us dry farmers in on the deal. Split our own shakes, get a load of lumber from the old mine for forms—won't cost us nothing but the cement."

Again Katie shoved Jackson's reluctant hand out to seal the bargain. Sid clung to the hand. "And of course I keep whatever I take out of the place. Get rid of your dirt and everything for you."

"Sure, Sid. That's good of you."

"Hey, the same goes for us!" Reed Carter cried.

"Oh, sure."

Katie couldn't hold it any longer. She burst into laughter. Sid guffawed. Reed and Young Merrill howled. Even Jackson, though bewildered, joined in the merry mirth; he felt warm toward these generous men, and they were so happy to be doing him a good turn that it made him happy too. Everybody shook hands around, and the three remodelers left. Watching them go, Katie began laughing all over again. She sat down on a box in the kitchen to enjoy it.

"Jack, if you fell in a lion's den you'd come out with a fur coat."

"Mighty fine fellows," Jackson said. "Didn't realize they liked me so much."

"Sometimes I don't know whether you're deep or just plain stupid. Don't you know what they're after?"

"What?"

"Treasure! Another cache like the one you found!"

"But—but, hell, there ain't any money ditched around here," Jackson said. "Where'd they get that idea?"

"Yes, I wonder. You've got twenty-five thousand dollars sticking out of your hind pocket."

"But—Grandpa Skinner never buried that money around here! I found it!"

"That," Katie pointed out, "is what makes it so funny."

CHAPTER
TWENTY-TWO

Jackson mulled it over. "But I told 'em somebody planted it on me. I put up a sign at the store about finding it."

"Yes, Jack. But nobody's going to believe anybody is sneaking in and planting a fortune on you."

"Don't you?"

"Jack, I'll be frank. Since yesterday morning nothing at all that you did or said or had happen to you is going to surprise me in the least. Yes, I believe it. I don't know how or why, but a lot of even stranger things are going on."

"I'm glad you're with me."

"I'm just with you that far. Don't leap at conclusions."

"Katie, I can't let those fellows fix up my place under those circumstances. It ain't fair."

"You shook hands on it, and don't try to back out. What's the difference, anyhow? The Carters and the Littlewalls and the dry farmers are all in cahoots. It won't cost any one person much—and a pity, too! It'll be a good lesson to them and it ought to come higher. Say," she said, "what if they *do* find something?"

They both laughed. He felt she was so pretty when she

was happy, teeth gleaming between the moist lips. He wanted her to be happy all her life.

"Katie!" Henry Brown's face was at the hole in the door.

"Got to fix that door," Jackson said.

"You're getting new doors," Katie reminded—"Come in, Henry."

Henry did, remembering to put his hand on his back. "Katie, this hardly looks right, you alone with him here."

"Such trust, Henry."

"It isn't that. It just doesn't look right. If you'll wait outside a minute, I want to talk to Jack. And then I'll talk to you."

"You'll talk to me where you find me," Katie said stiffly. "So long, Jack. See you at the wedding."

"You sure will," Jackson said.

Katie tossed her head and went out.

Henry sat down on the backless chair. He looked bad. He had done some very tall and some very deep thinking. All his vague fears of many years had come to a focus. He was facing disaster. His luck had run out. He had considered the implications of a fall from grace—an object of scorn, cut off from the Church, denied Katie, and possibly, confronted with the appalling extremity of prison. Not to mention financial chaos. He looked every day of his age, plus ten years. "Well?" he said, regarding Jackson with the rapt attention of a trapped animal.

"Must be hell when your back goes out like that," Jackson observed. "You look bad." He opened the drafts and poked some cedar in the stove. "I'll warm up the coffee—Coffee-Near."

"Coffee-Near? Don't you have the real stuff? I need it. Doctor's orders, you know."

"This is the nearest thing to coffee you ever tasted."

"It's not like that horrible jalap Ned Holt makes?" Henry drew a deep breath and made the plunge: "Jack, the country's in bad shape."

"Always has been, far's I can remember," Jackson agreed. "What I figure, emergency must be the normal state of affairs."

"It's the politicians. Bureaus and regulations. All those millions of mouths hanging on the public teats. We feed 'em, Jack. You and me. And after you've paid all the other taxes they take away what's left with the income tax. A man takes a risk with his investment and he works his fool head off, and they take it. He can't get a little ahead for his kids or provide for his old age. The dirty robbing politicians!"

"Sure a shame," Jackson admitted. "Me, I ain't had much trouble that way."

"That's what I'm getting at, Jack," Henry said hastily. This Jackson Whitetop was a sharp one. Henry threw back his head and made his great laugh. "Jack, you got a little surprise coming. You see, Jack, you was away to war and I had power of attorney to handle your affairs and I figured, well, now, here's Jack Whitetop, offering his life to his country, and what do the politicians do? They want to bleed you white while you're gone, with taxes. Jack, I wanted to go to war. I wanted to do my share. But they wouldn't have me. My back, you know."

"That so?" The way Jackson had heard it, Henry had angled frantically for a commission until the draft age was reduced, and then had refused the offer of a commission. Though Jackson didn't hold it against him. On the contrary, having been in the Army, Jackson felt that anybody who had kept out or wangled a good spot was doing the very smartest thing.

"And what could us civilians do except save fat and paper and drive slow to conserve tires? And then I seen a way to help out a little bit. Yes, sir; I seen a way to help at least one of the boys who was over fighting for his country. Maybe the politicians didn't appreciate him, but I did."

"Those combat boys had it rough," Jackson admitted.

"You sure did, Jack."

"Oh, me, I had a soft touch in headquarters."

Henry lowered his voice confidentially. "Jack, you didn't think I was serious yesterday about you owing me all that money?"

"If you wasn't, you sure did a good job of dead-panning. You said it was down in the books."

Henry threw back his head again for a great laugh. "Jack, that's for the record. Just for the record. We can't be too careful. Actually, Jack—" Henry's voice became a whisper— "actually, you made money during the war. Good money. Couldn't help it on sheep, a man like me running 'em. There were angles, Jack. Still are. Sheep are a gold mine if you know the angles."

"I'll be doggoned," Jackson said.

"I wish you hadn't flashed that package of money around, Jack. I know how you felt. You thought I was clipping you. I don't blame you. I was just having my little joke and you thought I meant it. If you'd just come to me and had a little private talk, we could have ironed things out between us."

"Oh. Then it's *your* money?"

Henry chuckled. "No, Jack. It's not mine. It's your money. Keep it."

"That's sure good of you, Henry. But what'll I tell folks?"

"Don't tell 'em anything. Or say it was phoney money. Or a joke. Or that you found it hidden in the house."

"That wouldn't be honest."

"Of course it's honest. It's your money, isn't it? You've got it coming fair and square. If you didn't give it to the politicians, whose business is that? A nest egg will come in handy, Jack, man getting married."

"That's sure true," Jackson admitted. "But I don't see how I got all this coming, if the books show I owe you nine thousand."

Henry chuckled. "Jack, books can show anything. Take hay. Charge a man labor and rent on equipment and so on, and there ain't a sheep in the world worth feeding through a hard winter. Take loss by storm and fire and flood—who can check up on it?"

"You can count the sheep."

Henry winked. "The sheep are gone, Jack. But that don't mean they're lost."

Jackson poured coffee. Henry tasted his and grimaced. "Not bad, Jack. But nothing takes the place of real coffee."

"If you faked the books for me, then I guess you done it on your own sheep, too."

"Well, now, Jack, there's no use going into that. I'm glad we had this little talk. Been going to see you about this ever since you got back. Sort of wanted to feel you out, first. You understand. Technically, it's against the law."

"That's the only trouble, Henry," Jackson said. "I guess I don't love taxes no more than the next one. But somebody's got to kick through and I'll do my share. If I got this money coming, I want it down in black and white on the books. What you do about your own affairs is your own business. I don't want any kickback on mine."

Henry set his coffee cup on a corner of the stove. "Jack, I can't do that. If I changed the books for your account, what would it do to me?"

"Should of thought about that in the first place."

"All right, Jack," Henry said. "What do you want?"

"I don't want nothing except what's coming to me."

"And then what?"

"Well, if I was a crook like you, I sure wouldn't try to marry a nice girl like Katie and get her tangled up in a mess."

"So that's it."

"That's about it."

"There's just one thing, Jack. Just one little thing. Maybe you know a lot about this, but you'd have a hard time getting a spirit into court to testify."

"Huh?"

"Just what can you prove? My books are in shape. Just where will you get in a showdown? Nobody's listening to us now. You can't prove where that package of hundred-dollar bills came from. I'm offering you a deal. Take it or leave it."

"Be seeing you around, Henry."

"O.K." Henry arose. "If you want it that way."

"Hey, don't forget this." Jackson pulled the big packet of bills from his pocket."

"Oh, no, Jack. I'm not that simple."

"What'll I do with it?"

"That's your baby." Henry went out.

Jackson shrugged and tossed the money on the drainboard. Funniest thing he ever saw, the way people wouldn't take money around here.

Henry drove back feeling some better. At least he knew where he stood, and his position wasn't really as bad as he'd imagined. He had, he felt, been more than generous. He had offered Jackson a cut and a good one. He'd gone to him man to man. If Jackson wouldn't talk business, if he thought he could put on the squeeze—well, that was just his tough luck. He couldn't prove anything, and Henry Brown hadn't spent a lifetime building a position to let it go without a fight. If Jackson thought it would be easy, well, Jackson simply didn't know the half of it.

But, still—what about this spirit business? The vague fear of the unknown gnawed at him. To hell with it, Henry told himself. A ghost couldn't scare him. But some mighty strange things had happened. Well, to hell with it.

When he reached the store, a green sedan was parked in front and two men were sitting on the edge of the porch. The two were entirely different in a way, one being short and wiry and the other tall and heavy. In another way they were curiously alike. They dressed alike and a bit too well, in double-breasted suits and snap-brim hats. The suits were a trifle snug and a trifle loud, their shoes had an incredible gloss, their socks and ties were slightly wild; but it was the eyes which made them alike. Eyes somehow a trifle too openly honest and steady.

"Closing up shop, Henry?" the big man asked.

"Shouldn't go off and leave a store like this," the little man said. "Dishonest men might break in."

The big man laughed as if this were very funny.

"Boys," Henry said, "you don't know how glad I am to see you."

"We just dropped by," the little man said. "We could use a hundred spring lambs."

"Don't want to crowd you, Henry," the big man said, "but we can make it awfully good business."

Henry laughed. "Don't make me laugh."

"Well, O.K., Henry," the little man said. "Maybe it is a little too soon, after what we got yesterday."

"Well, when could we take delivery?" the big man asked.

"Piker stuff," Henry said. "How would you like to pick up twenty-five thousand bucks nice and quick on a clean deal?"

The two men exchanged honest glances. "Quit twisting my arm," the big man said.

"All you've got to do is ask for the money. Simple as that."

"Hell, I can knock over a bank any day," the little man said. "It's not our line."

Henry had taken Jackson's notice from the store post. He got it from a pocket and handed it over. The two men studied it.

"Twenty-five G.'s," the big man mused. "He wants to give it away. Is he crazy?"

Henry threw back his head and laughed. "He tried to give it to me, but I wouldn't take it."

"Maybe you're crazy," the little man said.

"I left my crystal ball in my other pants," the big man said. "What's the deal?"

"All you've got to do is pick up. It's in hundreds. I can give you the serial numbers."

The little man asked, "How hot is this dough?"

"Perfectly good money. You ought to know. I got it from you."

"Oh," the little man said. "So that's where he found it."

"And naturally you don't like to claim it," the big man said. "You wouldn't. What's your cut?"

"It's all yours," Henry said. "It's worth that much to get rid of him."

"Oh, no," the little man said. "We don't go in for that, Henry. No rough stuff. But for money like that you won't have no trouble having it done. I got a friend who can arrange it."

"I don't mean kill him. I wouldn't want that. I wouldn't even want to see him hurt."

"Let's start from scratch, Henry," the big man said.

"You know the old Jonah Mine?"

"Sure."

"Say you took him out there on a deal to open it up for something and he had to walk back. Isn't that worth the money? It's no more than a practical joke, in a way."

"It's too *damned* easy," the little man said.

"Not when you understand things. This joker got into my private cache and now he's putting on the squeeze. But he's also due for a shotgun wedding this afternoon. If he isn't on deck for that wedding, he might just as well keep right on walking."

"Why, he wouldn't want to get married anyhow, under the circumstances," the little man said.

"He certainly doesn't," Henry admitted.

"So we'd be doing him a favor," the big man said.

"And he wants to get rid of the money anyhow," the little man said. "I always like to help a nice young fellow out."

CHAPTER TWENTY-THREE

Jackson cooked the weird ingredients of Ned Holt's coffee substitute in a frying pan. He put some in a coffee pot, brewed it, and tried a cup. It tasted like an old horse blanket, just as he'd expected. They all did. He hadn't much faith in a recipe that included such things as curly sage and a dash of greasewood.

He heard a car come in, and went out to find a green sedan containing two well-dressed strangers. The smaller of the two got out, and handed Jackson the notice from the porch post. "Hear you found the money that we lost."

"You lost it?" Jackson was surprised. He was sure it was Henry's money.

"Sure, we lost it. I kept a list of the serial numbers." The little man produced the list.

Jackson went inside and checked the list against half a dozen bills. Funniest thing he ever had happen to him. The money mysteriously appearing, Henry making out as if it was his but refusing to take it, and now these two strangers showing up to identify it. He figured there was something about it all he didn't understand, but at any rate it was off his hands now with a clear conscience. He took the money out and gave it to the stranger. "Here you go. I'm sure glad to get rid of this stuff."

The little man's eyes narrowed suspiciously. He'd expected at least an argument. This local yokel was either plenty dumb or plenty deep. "Thanks, friend. You're an honest man. They don't come like you that often."

"I don't want what ain't mine, is all. How'd the stuff get in my place in the first place, is what I can't figure out."

A deep one, the little man concluded, playing dumb. Couldn't come out and admit, of course, that he'd pinched it from Henry. "Well, friend, it beats me. But as long as we got it back, why worry?"

"That's how I figure."

"Well, let's go," the big man said from the car.

The little man turned to him. "Say, how about it?"

"How about what?"

"Here's some talent you don't find lying around every day."

"You got something there."

The little man turned to Jackson. "You know damned well this isn't our money, don't you, friend?"

"You identified it."

"That's the spirit. You know damned well it's Henry's dough, but you popped off your face and put up a sign, and when we come along with the numbers there's nothing else you can do but fork it over. You're a smart monkey, friend. You knew when to lay down two pairs against three aces. How'd you like to square up with Henry? How'd you like to have Henry where the hair is short?"

"I ain't got nothing against Henry," Jackson protested. "Except he beat me out of some money."

The two strangers laughed. "That makes you pals," the little man said. "Hop in, and we'll talk on the way."

"Where we going?"

"The old Jonah Mine."

"Jonah? What for?" The Jonah had been closed down since 1916.

"Look, friend. I don't like Henry no more than you do. And I had a son of my own who went overseas and never come back." The little man took off his snap-brim hat and put it over his heart.

"That's tough, mister," Jackson said. "You don't look that old."

"I lived a clean life, is why. My only boy gave his life for his country. And while you was over there in the muck and the mud—"

"I was in headquarters. We had it pretty soft."

"While you was over there fighting for your country, Henry Brown was robbing you blind. You heard about them sheep he lost yesterday, because Ned Holt had another of his spells?"

"I heard about it."

"Twenty of them sheep are yours, friend. They're up in the old Jonah tunnel, waiting to be picked up."

"Why, that dirty crook," Jackson said.

"I guess you just about got Henry where the hair's short. Hop in, friend. We can be there in a couple of hours."

It took, actually, almost three hours. The old road up Garrison Gulch was eroded, washes having formed at places in the tracks, and badgers had found it an ideal home. Except for an occasional sheep wagon, the road had seen no traffic since the Jonah closed down.

"Didn't know it would take so long," Jackson said. "I got

to be back."

"We'll only be there a few minutes," the little man said. "I know the man on guard. He's got no love for Henry. You talk to him and let him know who you are and what Henry's doing to you, and it's that simple. He'll walk away and we'll drop you off home and go get the sheriff."

"Kind of tough on Henry," Jackson said.

"If you break the law, friend, you got to take the consequences. Henry should of knowed that when he started his crooked work."

The car bumped around a turn of the gulch and the old dump came in sight, the tailing a huge pile on the mountainside. The old stamp mill was across the gulch, a crazy leaning structure half robbed away by people needing lumber. The car stopped below the tailing pile.

"I'll go up and see the guard," the little man said. "I'll holler when it's O.K." He scrambled up the loose tailings with the agility of a monkey, making a considerable clatter. He reached the top, far above, and disappeared. Presently he came in view on the rim and called down. "O.K., friend!"

Jackson scrambled up the tailings. The loose rock slid underfoot, and he paused, puffing, halfway to the top. He was certainly out of shape. From somewhere he heard the rattle of rock, and he wondered if the guard was already taking to the brush. Just as well. He didn't particularly want to know the crook. Wonderful, he felt, how everything was working out. With those sheep in the Jonah tunnel, Henry would be a Christian. All Jackson cared about was getting what was due him. Figured he'd talk the two strangers out of going for the sheriff. He had no desire to see Henry in jail. Just put it up to him, get the books straightened up, warn him that he'd better forget about entangling Katie—yes, it was all working out. Jackson cast an eye at the sun. Along noon or a little past. Ought to be back before Nephi returned from Tooele. Something had to happen on that. He certainly couldn't marry Anita. Well, have faith. It was working out somehow.

He started up again. Certainly was a climb to the top. He was wet with sweat and wheezing when he reached it. The little man was not in view, and Jackson followed the rusty ore-car tracks to the mouth of the tunnel. It was black inside. "Hey!" he yelled. It came to him he didn't know the name of the little man. "Hey!"

His voice came back hollowly from the blackness. He went back to the rim of the tailing pile. Below, the green sedan was a quarter mile down the gulch, bumping along faster than it should have been, considering the road. As it turned the shoulder of the hill he glimpsed the two men in it. One of them waved, and the car disappeared.

"I'll be go to hell," Jackson said. The little man obviously had scrambled down the other side while Jackson was climbing up. He cocked an eye at the sun. He was forty miles from home. Couldn't hope to get back, walking, before morning. By that time, there'd be no use showing up. Nephi would shoot him on sight.

He felt very much like a man holding a bag in one hand, a lantern in the other, and shouting for snipe.

There was no use trying to go back. The best thing was just to keep right on going.

CHAPTER
TWENTY-FOUR

Jackson sat down and got out tobacco. To hell with the Word of Wisdom and the whole shebang. He needed a smoke and he was tired of the whole deal. Nothing but trouble ever since Grandpa Skinner appeared.

"Jack!"

The voice seemed to come from nowhere. Jackson guiltily dropped his half-rolled cigarette and looked at the sky. If ever he needed a little help from beyond, this was it.

"Y-yes," he whispered. "Yes, G-grandpa—"

"Hey, Jack!"

It didn't sound, really, like a voice from beyond, this time. Somebody was yelling. He got up and looked about.

"Hey, Jack! Over here!"

Below and across the gulch a figure was waving beside the leaning structure of the old stamp mill.

"Sid! What the hell you doing here?"

"Getting a load of lumber for the concrete forms, like I said!" Sid Worth called. "Was they there when you left?"

"Who?"

"The dry farmers! They was going to start digging while I got the lumber!"

"Maybe they're there by now. Got your team?"

"How would I get here this quick in a team? My truck's inside!"

Jackson scrambled down the tailings and hurried across the gulch. Sid Worth, squatting against the wall of the stamp mill, regarded him quizzically.

"Sid, I never was so surprised to see anybody in my life."

"You sure jumped when I yelled, all right." Sid winked. "It's O.K., Jack. I know just how you feel. In your place I'd do the same thing."

"Those two jokers brought me up and run off without me!"

"Never mind, Jack. I won't say a word. Me, I wouldn't marry one of them Smith girls, neither, without a shotgun at my back."

"I've got to get back, Sid, or they'll think I run away."

"Imagine that. Anybody knows you wouldn't do a thing like that. Who was they? I seen the little guy skin up and make sure the coast was clear. Of course my truck's inside here and he didn't see it—"

"Sid, they tricked me."

"Sure they did. And a shame, too. You really wanted to hang around and get married up to Anita."

"You damn fool! I'm trying to tell you! They cooked up a story about—oh, hell," Jackson said. "Look, I don't give a damn what you think, but I've got to get back."

"Jack, I don't think I like that. We knowed each other a long time. When I tell you you can trust me, that ought to be enough."

"Do you want me to kick your fool teeth in? I tell you

I'm serious! Those guys tricked me. Some deal with Henry
to get me away so I couldn't go back."

Sid stood up. "Go to hell, Jack, if I don't figure you're
serious."

"How many times do I have to say it?"

"Then, hell, Jack, let's go."

The truck, an old Dodge with good clearance, wasn't
bothered at all by the high centers that had been such a
hazard to the green sedan. Sid simply took the road as it
came, and he overhauled the sedan near the mouth of the
gulch. Sighting the pursuit, the sedan speeded recklessly.

"Keep on their tails, Sid. I want a word with those
boys."

"What's the deal?"

Jackson explained, and Sid poured on the coal, crowding
the rear bumper of the sedan as the two vehicles bumped
along the narrow mountain road. "What I can't figure is
how they got the numbers of them bills," Sid said. Jackson
had left out part of the story, the part about Henry's visit.

The sedan reached the mouth of the gulch, and with
escape ahead took on a reckless burst of speed, drawing
away from the old truck. There was a crash, the sedan
shuddered, and as it sped on it left a trail of oil.

"We lost 'em," Jackson said.

"Won't be long now," Sid corrected.

The sedan sped across the sage flat. Smoke began pouring out behind, mixing with the dust. Sid chugged along
complacently. The sedan was two miles in the lead when it
stopped. Sid overhauled it and pulled alongside. The two
strangers sat silent.

"You forgot me," Jackson said.

"I half believe this angel stuff," the big man muttered. He tossed the packet of money to Jackson. "We noticed you left this in the car. We was going to drop it off at your house."

"The jig's up," Jackson said. "You better come clean. You cooked this whole thing up with Henry, to get me away. He gave you the numbers of the bills."

"Numbers?" the little man asked blankly.

"Numbers on what bills?" the big man asked blankly.

"Look, you want me to get tough?" Jackson said, his temper rising. He was getting tired of being shoved around. Grandpa Skinner might do it, but not these two jokers.

The two men looked at one another in amazement. "What's he talking about?" the big man asked the little man.

"Beats me," the little man said to the big man. "He asked us to drive him up to the old Jonah Mine and leave him there. We didn't know him from Adam, but what the hell? And now he starts in on numbers."

"Numbers on bills," the big man said. "Does he owe some bills?"

"So it's that way," Jackson said.

"You got the advantage of me, friend," the little man protested.

"If you'd tell us what it's all about—" the big man suggested.

"All right," Sid snapped, "then why was you trying to get away with the money?"

"Money?" The little man's eyes were wide. "What money?"

"This money you tossed to Jackson is what money."

"Money?" the big man said. "Is there money in that package? I thought it was a sandwich or something, which he left on the seat of the car when he got out at the mine. We was going to drop it off—"

Jackson sighed. "Let it go, Sid."

"Yeah; these guys have been questioned before."

"O.K., you two. Hop in and we'll ride you in."

"Thanks, friend," the little man said. The pair got out of the car, and suddenly broke into a run across the sage flat. "But if you don't mind," a voice floated back, "we'd rather walk!"

"Then let 'em walk," Sid said, and chugged along in the old Dodge.

Jackson chuckled. "I guess they're what you'd call too smart for their own good. They'll find out."

When the truck pulled into Jackson's place a swarm of men were at work. The roof dirt had been shoveled off, the floors torn up, and the canvas lining ripped from the log walls. A big pile of rubbish was blazing, and so was an argument between the ranchers and the dry farmers.

"Jack," Young Merrill Littlewall cried, "you're just the man we want to see! We agreed to put in the floors. Ain't that so?"

"Well, yes."

"Not so fast!" a dry farmer cried. "We agreed to put in the basement. You shook hands on that!"

"You sure did," Sid Worth said. "What's the trouble?"

"They're trying to dig the basement!" the dry farmer cried.

"You dirty crooks!" Sid exclaimed.

Young Merrill placed a hand on Jackson's arm. "Jack, we're only trying to do a first-class job. According to the city building code, a man's got to have eighteen inches clearance under his floors. We're putting in the floors, and it's our job to excavate that clearance."

"That's right!" Reed Carter said. The ranchers echoed agreement.

"Clearance!" Sid Worth emitted a yelp of pain. "Anything under the floors is basement!"

"Not for eighteen inches it ain't. It's clearance. That's the code."

"Code and be damned! This ain't no city and there ain't no code!"

"You can see we're only trying to do a good job, Jack," Young Merrill said, "if they'll let us."

"All I done is just let out the contracts," Jackson said. "I'm not bossing the job. Settle it among yourselves."

Sid asked a dry farmer: "Anything in the roof dirt?"

"Not a dime. And the ranchers didn't find nothing behind the canvas. And now the crooks are trying to beat us out of excavating the foundation!"

"You can excavate," Young Merrill said, "after we've dug the clearance. Eighteen inches."

"And who's a crook?" Reed Carter asked.

"Who's putting in the foundation?" Sid said. "Let me ask you that."

"O.K. Well, it's a fine foundation that don't stick up high enough to give eighteen inches clearance under the floor. We already got plans figured for a two-foot foundation. The floors will be two feet off the ground after we jack up the house. You can excavate all you want from there on down eighteen inches."

The ranchers were glum. The dry farmers beamed.

A Model T, its approach unnoticed in the argument, rattled up. Anita was at the wheel, old Nephi grim beside her with his .30-30 across his knees.

"All right, Jack," Nephi said. "Let's go. You're getting married up."

"Got the license?" Young Merrill asked.

"Sure I got the license," Nephi said and produced it.

"But I thought Jackson and Anita would have to apply for it in person. Ain't that the law?"

"Don't you think I know the law, with all the marrying off I've done?"

"Well, ain't it?"

"I have found," Nephi said, "from long experience that it's best to appear at a young man's house with a gun *and* the license. It's quick and clean, that way, and he don't have time to change his mind. Anyhow, on a long trip to Tooele and back if the boy was along I might get so worked up I'd shoot the rat, and then where'd my girl be? So I always get the license personally. I want to know it's right."

"But how do you get it?" Young Merrill persisted.

"Sign the boy's name, of course," Nephi said scornfully.

CHAPTER
TWENTY-FIVE

There was an embarrassed silence as Jackson climbed into the car. "Fixing up the house real nice," Sid Worth said brightly, "for the bride and groom."

"We're doing the fixing up," Young Merrill corrected. "The dry farmers is just fiddling with a roof and basement."

"Full basement," Sid said proudly.

"Well isn't that nice?" Anita said.

Reed Carter said, "We're putting in a bathroom and new floors and finishing up the inside."

"And closets," Young Merrill added. "Big closets."

Anita beamed. "That's marvelous."

Nephi Smith was touched. "That's real good of you boys. Coming to the wedding, I suppose?"

"Well, we ain't dressed for it," Reed Carter said, glancing suspiciously at the dry farmers.

"Just come as you are. We all know everybody hereabouts. I always like a good wedding for my girls. And I ain't had one yet. Come as you are." He winked, indicating a barrel between the front and back seats, on which Jackson had perched his feet. "Got a barrel of cider along. Real shindig."

"Well," Sid Worth said, "if we *all* went." His manner indicated that he didn't want to catch any ranchers digging that foundation while he was gone.

The wedding party made a considerable convoy. "We'll pull in at the store and invite Henry," Nephi said.

"By all means," Anita said. "Henry's got to be there."

Henry was sitting on the porch with his chair tilted back and his feet high against a post, feeling very pleased with the world, when the convoy pulled in.

"Hi, Henry," Anita said. "We're all going to the wedding."

"Jump in, Henry," Nephi invited. "Plenty of room."

"Sit right here beside me," Jackson said.

Henry's feet hit the floor with a thump, and then he grabbed his back. He leaned forward, staring at Jackson.

"You shouldn't do things like that, Henry," Anita said. "Not with your back. Not at your age."

"Well, don't sit there like a bump on a log, Henry," Nephi said. "Git in."

Henry arose, and like an automaton wobbled to the Model T.

"Some friend of yours called on me," Jackson said. "Nice fellows in a green car. Showed me the old Jonah. Hadn't been up there since before I went to war."

Henry got in, slumped against the cushions, and put his feet on the cider barrel.

"Sid Worth brought me back," Jackson said. "Sid was up getting some lumber for concrete forms."

Henry gazed ahead stupidly, unseeing. The conviction was growing that he was fighting fate. Whatever he did was wrong. Nothing panned out any more. His luck had turned.

The bishop came out as the convoy pulled into his place.

"Ready, Bishop?" Nephi asked happily.

"Er—I thought we could have the ceremony in my office," the bishop suggested. He believed in a simple, private ceremony in such cases. "Just big enough for the bride and groom and witnesses."

"To hell with that, Bishop. Everybody's waiting up at my place now. Womenfolks cooking a big feed and all. This here's an occasion."

The bishop coughed. "Don't you think a quiet little ceremony—"

"Hell, no," Nephi said flatly. "It's my own daughter, ain't it? She's got her man, ain't she? What's wrong with that? Better late than never, I say. Been worried about my Anita girl, but she's got her a man and that's what counts. It's a big day for me. Bring Sister Jensen along, too. And Katie."

"I'll get my Bible." The bishop went into the house. Katie and Sister Jensen were peering out the front curtains.

"We might as well all go," the bishop said. "Where's my Bible?"

"In your office. I certainly wouldn't be caught dead at such an affair," Sister Jensen said.

"That's not the right spirit."

"And I'm sure Katie has too much pride, too."

"Oh, I wouldn't miss it for a million," Katie said, rushing to her room. "Be ready in a minute, Dad!"

"Beryl," the bishop said.

"You really want me to go?"

"Beryl, I'm troubled. Sorely troubled." The bishop paused, glancing toward the door of Katie's room, and lowered his voice. "Beryl, there's a matter I've spoken of to nobody. Young Jack Whitetop came to me the other morning good grief, I guess it was only yesterday; so much has happened. And he spoke to me on a very serious matter."

"You mean about his visitation?"

"How did you know about that?"

"Why, I—it's around, Waldo. It's gossip. Milo Ferguson claims old Moroni Skinner appeared to him, and Jackson has been acting strange. People say he had a visitation too."

"Yes, he did. About a matter that sorely tried me. I prayed for guidance, and—Beryl, I received a message. A voice spoke to me from beyond. And now it can't transpire. What can I think? What am I to believe? What faith can I cling to?"

At this solemn moment, Nephi's voice came harshly: "Shake a leg, Bishop! You're holding things up!"

"Don't get your shirt off!" the bishop cried— "Beryl, I'm all at loose ends. All my life I've held faith. Through thick and thin. But now I've had a message. I've heard a voice. And things aren't working out. They just can't. What can I do?"

"You're upset, poor dear," Beryl Jensen said soothingly. "What's happened and all. Poor Henry and his back. You must hold faith, Waldo. It's not for us to question the ways of the Lord. He moves in a mysterious way."

"Doggone mysterious," the bishop mumbled. "Jackson will be married off to Anita inside an hour."

Beryl Jensen was mightily troubled, also. Her little ruse of speaking into the milk can had been a thing of momentary impulse. Only afterward had she begun to realize the incalculable effect on her husband. She wondered if it would destroy his faith and ruin his life, and this thought brought back her resentment against Jackson. She didn't believe any part of Jackson's claim to having had a visitation. She'd been fighting fire with fire. But her husband's faith had been a rock to anchor to, and now she wondered if it were dissolving. The bishop had been a happy man, and happy men aren't too common. He'd been serene in the knowledge that his was the faith that made for the best possible life on earth and the greatest glory in the hereafter. And now her ruse threatened to shatter it all.

If she told him it was only a cheap trick on her part, what would happen? Would it be the end of all between her and him? Could he ever forgive such an act? And if she didn't what would happen? Milo Ferguson and Nephi Smith had turned apostate for less. Too, if she told him, what could he ever believe in the future? Her voice echoing hollowly from the milk can was to him something from beyond; his belief in it had given him every feeling he would have experienced if it had been an actual spirit speaking. Could he, knowing, ever take anything of like nature seriously again? Would he begin doubting all voices and visitations? Would he scoff at Joseph Smith and the golden plates?

"Waldo—"

"Here's your Bible, Dad," Katie said, bursting in. "It was in my room. Are you ready?"

"You go out and tell them I'll be a minute."

"O.K."

"Yes, Beryl?" the bishop asked his wife.

"Just—keep the faith, Waldo," Beryl Jensen said pleadingly. "Don't give up your faith, whatever happens." She couldn't tell him.

CHAPTER
TWENTY-SIX

The bishop went out. "Well, where's your wife?" Nephi cried. "Tell her we ain't got all day!"

"Sister Jensen doesn't feel too well."

"All right, climb in."

At the mouth of East Canyon the cars picked a way among the boulders left by the old flood, and Jackson, seeing the splintered stubs of weathered lumber and the rock-like gray humps of hardened cement, was reminded dismally of the bishop's requirements. Take some doing to settle the Trouble.

Jackson felt that he had faith enough, but it seemed that the fulfillment of Grandpa Skinner's command just couldn't be. Anita, between Katie and Nephi in the front, was chipper as a canary, and Jackson felt like wringing her neck for her. Nephi was beaming. At any rate, Jackson's misery had company in the rear. Henry was certainly not happy, and the bishop's face was bleak and perplexed.

The cars came out of the jumbled wash left by the flood and climbed the benchland. The Smith house was set among a grove of trees watered by a spring. It was a two-story eyesore of weathered lumber, a few faint traces of the original red paint here and there. Cars and rigs were in the yard, a couple of dozen kids chasing each other around, and the womenfolk had set up a big table for the wedding feast under a locust tree.

"What a wedding," Nephi said fondly. "My last daughter, and I'm really doing it up brown for her."

"Dad, you're so good to me," Anita said.

There was a whoop as the convoy drove up, and everybody rushed out to shake hands with Jackson and Anita. "My boy, my boy!" Nephi's young wife said fondly, embracing Jackson. Nephi's young wife was an ample woman in her late forties, though she appeared to be ten years older, as if she were trying to close the gap between herself and her husband. She clung to Jackson's neck and burst into happy tears. "We're so glad to have you in the family, Jack, my boy! I know you and Nita and little Henry will be so happy! Call me Mother. . ."

"All ready, everybody?" the bishop said brusquely.

"Oh, Nita, you're not dressed yet!" her mother cried. The womenfolk bustled Anita into the house to fix up. Jackson wanted a word with Katie, for whatever good it would do, but she went in with the other women. The men got the barrel out of the car and set it on a box under a tree. The bishop sat down on the lawn and looked at his watch.

"Jackson, I'm troubled."

"Me, too."

"Here you go," Nephi said, coming from the barrel with two brimming cans which, originally, had each held a quart of motor oil.

"What is it?" the bishop asked.

"Cider."

"Sweet cider?"

"Here, take it."

The bishop took a sip. "Hmm. Very refreshing."

Jackson took a swallow. The cider had a needle as big as a twenty-penny spike. He felt he needed a needle and what the bishop in his innocence didn't know wouldn't hurt him. The bishop drank his quart down thirstily and handed the can back to Nephi.

"Got plenty?"

"All you can take," Nephi said in amazement. He went to the barrel and brought the can back full, handed it to the bishop, and hurried away as if not to be responsible for what happened. Henry Brown, Jackson noticed, was well into his second quart; he suspected Henry might be able to take it better.

Nephi's young wife came out of the house toting Anita's child. "Jack dear, I know you want to get acquainted with little Henry. Isn't he the sweetest thing? Henrykins, say hello to Daddy." The child glared sullenly at Jackson. "This is your daddy, sweetheart. Don't you know your own daddy? Say hello to Daddy!"

"Mrs. Smith," the bishop said. His voice was strangely loud; one eyebrow was high and the other was low. "Haven't you got the common decency to keep that brat out of sight?"

"Why, Bishop Jensen! After all, I can introduce the child to its own father!"

"The whole thing is in bad taste. The whole damned thing. Very bad taste. Keep that brat out of sight. At least until after the ceremony. Let's try to pretend, at least, that this whole thing isn't a travesty on the holy ceremony of wedlock."

"Well, I declare!" Mrs. Smith declared. Her lower lip trembled and she turned to her husband. Silence had fallen over the happy throng of merrymakers. Nephi strode over from the cider barrel.

"Here, here. What's wrong here?"

The child began to bawl. "I don't think the bishop has any right talking to me like that and I don't care who he is!" Nephi's young wife blubbered, clutching the child to her ample bosom. "And he's frightened little Henry. You've no right to do that to an innocent child!"

"I merely told her," the bishop said loudly, "that this whole thing is in bad taste. I merely suggested that she keep that little bastard out of sight until after the ceremony."

"Little what?" Nephi bristled. "What did you say? Don't you go calling no names around here, Waldo Jensen!"

"I didn't call nobody no name," the bishop roared. "That's a technical term. Look it up."

"Don't get technical when we're trying to have a good time. I know what you said."

"A bastard," the bishop explained, "is a child without a father. That's not a name; it's what it is."

"Well, I never," Nephi's young wife said, bustling away.

"What do you mean, a child without no father?" Nephi demanded. "Every child has got a father. Otherwise it's a miracle, and I don't take no stock in miracles."

"When the father," the bishop said with strained patience, "is unknown."

"Unknown? He's sitting right there aside you big as life!"

"When," the bishop said, "he ain't married to the mother."

"What d'you think *you're* here for?"

"Go away," the bishop said. "I certainly won't get into a brawl over a technicality. Let's get the whole business over and done with."

"Since you apologized like a man, I'll accept it," Nephi said. He looked around. "Where'd my wife go? Here, you," he said to one of his sons-in-law, "go on in and tell the women to keep that little bastard out of sight until after the ceremony." Nephi, his honor appeased, strode to the barrel.

The bishop sighed and took a deep swig from his can. "Jackson, this ain't working out at all. The whole damned thing's in a mess."

"Yes, sir," Jackson said, wondering if he could somehow knock the bishop's hand and spill the rest of the cider.

The bishop cocked a glassy eye. "Jack, tell me something, man to man. Did Moroni Skinner *really* appear to you?"

"Yes, he did."

"Damn it! And did he tell you to marry my Katie?"

"That's right."

The bishop set down his can. It overturned. He spread his hands helplessly. "Then why is this happening?"

"Beats the hell out of me. Bishop, can I ask you a question?"

"Go ahead."

"Did you really hear a voice tell you that I was to settle the Trouble?"

"That's the worst of it. I did. I was asking for guidance and a voice spoke up just as plain as I'm talking to you now. Plainer, in fact. My tongue seems thick, or something. It's a warm day. I never should have called that kid a bastard, even if it is. I'm all upset, I guess. The voice told me that before you married Katie you'd have to settle the Trouble. Jack, that's what has me worried and puzzled. I've lived as good a life as I could. I worked for the gospel and I been the bishop here for a long time. And then at last I get a sign. A voice talked to me from beyond. And here we are. A forced marriage. Katie wouldn't marry you, after this, if you lived to be a thousand. And Apostle Black is mighty poorly, I hear. I still remember the day of the flood, and him telling us that he was inspired to say he'd dedicate our new meetinghouse. And it can't work out. A man's got to have faith, but I'm troubled."

The bishop gazed at the men around the cider barrel. Then he turned to eye the parked cars. Then he looked at Jackson speculatively.

Jackson shook his head. "It wouldn't work. Nephi would chase me down and shoot me like a dog. If I got away it wouldn't settle nothing. I couldn't come back."

"It's a test of faith," the bishop said glumly. "We've got to have faith. But it isn't easy, sometimes."

CHAPTER
TWENTY-SEVEN

The women came out of the house, twittering, with Anita. She was all dressed up and she was a very pretty girl.

"She'll make you a good wife," the bishop said.

"How do I look?" Anita asked, turning slowly before Jackson.

"I could wring your neck."

"Now, Jackson," the bishop reproved. "Any man should be glad to get such a pretty girl."

"O.K., Bishop!" Nephi cried. "Let's git it over with. I'm hungry!"

The bishop began getting up from the grass, and lurched forward. Jackson steadied him. "Legs must of gone to sleep," the bishop muttered. Jackson deftly swung a chair into position and the bishop thankfully clutched the back of it for support. "I feel fine," he muttered in an aside to Jackson. "I feel wonderful. Never felt better in my born life. But my legs are wobbly."

Katie, who'd come out with Anita, glared at Jackson. "A fine thing!" she said. "This is all your fault! Dad, are you all right?"

"I'm marvelous, Katie. Legs must of gone to sleep."

Jackson gripped the bishop's arm. "Maybe you'd better get the blood circulating." He led the bishop out among the trees.

Watching, Nephi chuckled. "Well, I'll be danged. He's human after all."

"You shouldn't of done that to him," Henry said. "He doesn't know what's the matter."

Nephi cocked an eye at Henry's can. "What do you mean? What's the matter, Brother Henry?" he asked innocently.

"Doctor's orders," Henry said. "My back. Doctor said an occasional stimulant—"

"Oh, for heaven's sake, Henry," Anita said, "why don't you just admit you like a snort now and then and be done with it?"

"You mealy-mouthed bigots make me sick," Nephi said, heading for the barrel.

"I'm going to sample that so-called cider," Katie declared firmly, following.

Anita said, "Henry, don't you think it's about time to be a man?"

"I washed my hands of the whole business long ago."

"You'll stand by and see another man railroaded?"

"It's your business. You claimed he was father of your brat. Why blame me?"

"I didn't say any such of a thing. And Henry's not a brat. I never said that Jackson was his father."

"You sure spread on impression."

"It was an impulse. They were riding poor Jack on a rail. He might have been injured for life. It just came to me. So

I grabbed up little Henry and ran out, and it saved him. I never did say Jack was the father. I remember exactly what I said. I told him to kiss little Henry good-bye. Then I said to ride all three of us out on a rail. Dad asked me if Jack was the father, and I said not to ask me such a question. And I distinctly said I wouldn't marry Jack Whitetop if he was the last man in the world. And I won't."

"For a girl who's lived as long as you have around your father," Henry observed, "you sure don't know Nephi Smith."

"Is that all the faith you've got, Henry?"

"Faith? What's faith got to do with it?"

"You know very well that Jackson's grandfather appeared to him and told him he'd marry Katie Jensen. So I couldn't possibly marry him."

"I see," Henry said slowly. He shook his head. "It won't work."

"Henry, I thought you'd be man about it. I never dreamed you'd let Jack go through with it."

"I done the right thing by you, and I washed my hands of the whole affair."

"That's what you think."

"Don't try to scare me. You won't get no place now, trying to change your mind about who's the father."

"You're such an utter heel, Henry. Do you think I've been scared by your threats to have little Henry taken away if I made trouble? I could have forced you to marry me any day I wanted to. I've got your letters. And what about my landlady in Salt Lake? Mrs. Toolson. She could have *made* you, any day of the week. But I'm waiting, Henry. I want to be asked. I don't want any man who doesn't want me."

"I think I need some more cider," Henry said.

"It's wonderful," the bishop said, as he came back with Jackson. "Exercise and deep breathing. Amazing how it puts strength into a man. I've never tried it before."

"Nothing like it, Bishop. I used to walk Pa around when he needed it."

"Think I'll take another drink of that delicious cider."

"I guess you won't," Nephi cried, overhearing. "Get the marrying over with first, and then I don't care what happens to you."

Everybody gathered around, and the bishop directed Jackson and Anita to stand before him holding hands. From far off came the blasting of an automobile horn.

"Somebody's coming," Jackson said. "I guess we better wait until they get here."

"We don't want anybody to miss out," Anita said. Her sublime faith was evidently a bit shaken.

"I guess we won't," Nephi declared. "I never invited 'em nohow, whoever they be. And anyhow the cider's getting low. Go ahead, Bishop."

"We are brought together here for the purpose of joining this man and this woman in the bonds of holy matrimony," the bishop said. "I wish they'd quit blowing that confounded horn. Where was I? Jackson Whitetop, repeat after me: I, Jackson, do take Anita—"

Jackson hesitated. Nephi prodded him from behind none too gently.

"I, Jackson, do take Anita—"

"Confound that horn."

"Confound that horn."

"Jackson, for goodness' sakes."

"Jackson, for goodness' sakes."

"Bishop, I want your regular ceremony," Nephi objected.

"It's that confounded horn. Getting louder and louder."

"You're cutting it short anyhow. I want your long cere-mony." Nephi was shouting, because the noise of the horn had become a bellow. Henry's weapons carrier bounced into view with Milo Ferguson grimly at the wheel with a dead cigar clamped in his jaws. Beside him, clinging on desperately, was a gray-haired woman, disheveled, hat awry, and covered with dust.

"Well, for goodness' sakes," Anita said. "It's Mrs. Toolson."

Milo skidded to a stop. "Git here on time?"

"Dang near too late," Nephi said. "The wedding's just started."

Mrs. Toolson climbed groggily from the vehicle. "A madman. Good heavens, what a ride!"

"Anything refreshing?" Milo asked.

Nephi jerked a thumb at the cider barrel. Milo drifted toward it, licking dusty lips. Anita said, "Are you all right, Mrs. Toolson? It must have been a hard ride."

"Why, you're no more sick than I am, Mrs. Brown," Mrs. Toolson said. "Kidnapped, that's what. Kidnapped."

"Sick? Of course I'm not sick."

"Kidnapped. He said you were sick and calling for me. And I came clean from Salt Lake for nothing. How's little Henry?"

"Oh, he's fine."

"And your husband? How's Mr. Brown?"

"Huh?" Nephi yelped.

"Oh, isn't that your husband running toward the car?" Mrs. Toolson said, pointing to Henry. Henry was indeed in a great hurry, so great that he chose for escape the first car he came to, which was Nephi's old Model T. He leaped into it and began stomping on the starter button.

"Ain't no battery," Nephi called. "If you can start it without jacking up the hind wheel, you're a better man than I am."

"Have I said something wrong?" Mrs. Toolson asked.

"Damn!" Anita said. "I didn't want it this way. Why didn't Milo mind his own business? Henry would have come through. I know he would."

"Who is this woman?" Nephi demanded.

"Mrs. Toolson was my landlady in Salt Lake."

"Oh, heavens, I forgot," Mrs. Toolson said. "It was a secret marriage, and I promised not to tell."

"You're married a'ready?" Nephi said.

"Maybe I've said too much," Mrs. Toolson said. "But when I saw you here, and your husband, I supposed you'd announced it. Especially since the baby came."

"Nita, are you married to Henry?" Nephi demanded.

"Well, all except the formality of a ceremony," Anita admitted demurely. "Who else?"

Nephi bristled. "Who else? Was there others?"

"And just who are you to be talking that way about this sweet little girl?" Mrs. Toolson demanded.

"I'm only her father. Who else, I want to know!"

"A fine father you are! There was nobody else! I ought to know. There's one thing I'll have you understand. Anita is as fine a girl as ever rented an apartment from me. Not like some I could mention, gallivanting around. I can tell you right now she was true to her husband. Home every night with a good book, unless Mr. Brown was in town."

"Henry!" Nephi called in a voice of terrible sweetness. "Oh, Henry!"

Henry climbed from the car and walked slowly to his doom. "Anita, dear. There is one thing I've been wanting to ask you."

"Why, what is it, Henry?" Anita said, the picture of innocence.

"Will you marry me?"

"Good heavens!" Mrs. Toolson cried. "Mr. Ferguson! Mr. Ferguson!"

"What d'you want?" Milo answered from the cider barrel.

"Mr. Ferguson, I would like to leave right away, please! This is no place for a woman of principle!"

"Any time you want," Milo said.

"I'll go, too," Katie said quietly.

"Guess there's no use me hanging around no more," Jackson said.

"Oh, Henry, this is so sudden," Anita said. "I've got to have time to think it over."

"Of course she'll marry you, you fool!" Nephi said to Henry. "Nita, why for you said it was Jackson?"

"I never did say it was Jack. You jumped at conclusions, and I hope this is a lesson to you. I was just trying to save him from the mob that night."

"I got a mind to turn you over my knee and spank your

bottom good. What if we'd married you up to Jackson? That wouldn't of been right."

"Oh, I knew Henry would be a man at the last moment. I've been waiting all along for him to ask me. After all, I have my pride."

"But what if he hadn't of?"

"But he did," Anita pointed out with a woman's logic. "I had faith. And after all, I was getting tired of waiting on Henry. I had to do something to prod him along. Jack's going to marry Katie. He had a visitation that told him so. The trouble with you, Dad, is that you don't have faith. You're an apostate."

"Visitation! Fiddlesticks! Rats!" Nephi cried, beyond his depth. "Damnation! And now I ain't even got a marriage license . . . Bishop, how about changing the names?"

"As I understand the law," the bishop said, "a couple who've been living together as man and wife can go to any minister of the gospel and get married without a license. It's for the purpose of privacy, to save embarrassment— Henry, you and Anita hold hands—That's right—Now, we are gathered here again for the purpose of joining this man and this woman—"

CHAPTER
TWENTY-EIGHT

Milo drove cautiously on the return trip. Mrs. Toolson was between him and Jackson, and the single seat made it necessary for Katie to sit on Jackson's lap, which thrilled him to the core.

"I hope the old fool's satisfied," Milo growled.

"Nephi don't care, so long as *somebody* marries Anita," Jackson pointed out.

"I ain't talking about Nephi. I mean Moroni Skinner, the old fool, messing around in my affairs. Danged near busted my fool neck a-saving you'n. If you need any more saving, you can do it yourself. I'm done."

"I sure appreciate it. How'd you know where to find Mrs. Toolson?"

"Why, I've lived in that same house forty year and better," Mrs. Toolson pointed out with fine logic. "My husband built it for me when we were married, and I've never lived anywhere else since. It was as fine a house as you'd find on Second South, and after he passed away I cut it up into apartments."

"I'm the postmaster, ain't I?" Milo said. "Henry and Anita was writing each other while she was in Salt Lake, and he had a awful lot of business in there for a spell. And then he sent her a special delivery letter with a two-hundred-dollar money order, and didn't have no more business in Salt Lake. And when Anita come back she had the baby. A man can add two and two."

"My house has always had a good name," Mrs. Toolson said. "I certainly wouldn't have allowed such goings on, if I'd suspected in the slightest way. But how was I to know? They said they were married."

At the bishop's place, Katie hopped out. "See you later, honey," Jackson said.

"I'll never speak to you again as long as I live!" Katie hurried inside.

"Lovers' quarrels," Mrs. Toolson said, smiling fondly at Jackson. Milo drove to the store, and ushered her into Henry's spare bedroom for the night; it was too late to start back for Salt Lake.

"Milo," Jackson said as the car was going down the valley, "do you know anything about a package I found on top my syrup can this morning?"

Milo puffed furiously at his cigar. "Quit twisting my arm."

"Why did you want to do a thing like that to me for?"

"It was your money. Henry owed it to you. And old Moroni Skinner appeared to me. Wouldn't be no other reason except that I was supposed to help you out. What do you know about Henry?"

"I know he's been gypping me. He admitted it."

"You squared up with him?"

"No way of proving he said it."

"I guess I'm just a nosy old coot, Jack. I keep his books for him, and they're straight. But it was damned funny to me how he's been the only man in the United States these past few years who always lost money on his sheep. And Henry couldn't saw a board straight to save his neck. He got men in to fix the house up after he took over from me. But he'd no more than moved in when he was a-hammering and sawing at nights. Took me quite a spell to figure it out. Henry was off gallivanting in Salt Lake quite a considerable, and it give me time. Finally I found the strongbox under the floor of his living room. Then I had to get a key. I always say where there's a will there's a way. It was his back.

"When his back goes out he can't tie his shoes. Can't bend over. Can't lift his feet up. Must be awful. So he'd get me to put his shoes on in the morning and I see the rawhide string on his neck. Well, Henry and me used to play a lot of cards at night, before he got converted and started chasing Katie most every night. Cribbage; and a couple of drinks. I fixed him up some stiff ones one night and had to put him to bed, and so pretty soon I had a key of my own like the one hanging from that string around his neck. And after that I seen that every time Henry lost some more sheep one way or another, there'd be some new hundred-dollar bills in that strongbox under the floor."

"You're a snooping old reprobate, Milo."

"Hell, ain't got much else to do. Sort of a hobby, I reckon. So you see, Jack, I kind of kept rough track of things, and I know what you got a-coming. Figuring everything and a little for interest, that money's your'n, with a little extra to boot as a lesson to him. Pay off what he's got against you on the books, it ain't too much."

"I don't want it like that. If I've got it coming, I want it on the books in black and white."

"That's appreciation, after what I done for you!" Milo declared. "Henry ain't a-going to change no books. It would be his neck. Take it and shut up about it. Say, what's going on here?" Milo asked, as he turned into Jackson's lane. "Looks like a cyclone's hit the place."

"Fixing it up a little for me and Katie."

"Got a hard row there, boy. She's sore at you for tripping up Henry. Sort of makes a fool out of her. And you got the bishop drunk. Look, Jack, just keep that money and don't say nothing to nobody."

"I've been trying to find out who owned it. Everybody knows I've got it."

"Oh, hell," Milo said. "Well, from now on you can do what you damn well please. I done enough, Moroni Skinner or no Moroni Skinner. I ain't no errand boy for no spirits. I don't even believe in spirits."

The happy newlyweds brought the bishop home in Nephi's Model T. Henry shook him awake and the bishop grimaced. "I think it's the heat," he said. "I feel awful."

Sister Jensen met her husband at the door. She hadn't been an English barmaid for nothing. "My head's whirling," the bishop groaned. "I don't know what come over me. I think I'm going to be sick."

"Oh, Waldo. Here, go in the bathroom and get rid of it. I'll fix you some strong coffee."

"Some Coffee-Near."

"Yes, Waldo." She went into the jam closet and got the can of coffee hidden for medical purposes. There was hot water on the stove and she put two cups of water into a saucepan and five heaping tablespoons of coffee. And she did some thinking. If Waldo had taken to drink because of what she'd done, the only thing to do was confess her duplicity. It might shake his faith, but the truth always was best.

When the bishop returned to the kitchen his face was dead white with a slight tinge of green about the edges. His wife ushered him into a chair. "Sit down. Here, drink this." The coffee was black as midnight.

"Where's Katie?"

"Never mind. She feels terrible. So humiliated."

The bishop sipped the coffee. "This hits the spot. I wish I could get Jackson to let me handle it."

"Yes, dear . . . Waldo?"

"Huh?"

"Waldo, I've got to tell you something."

"Can't it wait, the way I feel?"

"You've got to know, Waldo. I—I've deceived you."

The bishop's coffee cup clattered on the saucer. "What?"

"I deceived you, Waldo."

"I don't believe it. I can't believe it."

"I think it best to tell you everything, Waldo."

The bishop put his elbows on the table and his face in his hands. "No," he said. "No."

"The truth is always best."

"Wait a minute." He got up and shut the kitchen door. "You sure Katie's in her room? We don't want her to know."

"She already knows. Part of it."

The bishop groaned. He took a gulp of coffee, lifting the cup with two shaking hands. "You might have kept it from her."

"I did it for her sake."

"For her sake? You mean, you *told* her for her sake."

"Well, both."

"Why did you have to tell me? I was happy." The bishop took a deep breath. "Well, who is he?"

"Who's who?"

"Who's the man?"

"What man?"

"I've got a right to know. If I'm not Katie's father, then who is?"

Sister Jensen caught her breath. Her hand flew to her mouth defensively as if he'd hauled off and popped her one. "Waldo, I declare!" She burst into tears. "Waldo! I'll leave! I'll go away! You can't accuse me of that!"

"Well, what are you talking about, then?"

"I merely said I deceived you."

"When I went to school that meant something."

"Oh, Waldo, how could you? After all these years! I've been a good wife. I left green England for this godforsaken desert where it never rains. I've stood by you in thick and thin, and you've never trusted me! Why was I ever born?"

"Now, Beryl, that's not true. You said you deceived me, and what was I to think? It was a terrible shock. You mean you fooled me on some little thing? Tucking away money or something? Women always do that, Beryl."

"But it's worse than that," she sobbed. "The jam closet—

it's right next to your office. I always listen when you're in there with people."

The bishop chuckled encouragingly. "Well, after all, we're man and wife. We've no secrets between us. Though I never wanted to worry you over business affairs."

"And I heard what that scalawag told you—that Jackson Whitetop. That cock-and-bull story about Moroni Skinner appearing and telling him to marry Katie. That's simply not true, Waldo. If you wasn't so firm in the faith you'd know it in a minute."

"I was inclined to doubt it under the circumstances. But I asked for guidance and a voice told me it was true."

"Waldo, that was my voice."

"A voice spoke to me as plain as I'm speaking now. It said that before Jackson married Katie, he had to prove himself be settling the Trouble."

"It was my voice, Waldo."

"What? What did you say?"

"That was my voice. I was in the jam closet. I made my voice low and talked into the milk can."

"For heaven's sake, Beryl! You can't joke about a thing like that!"

"Go into your office, Waldo. I'll do it again."

When the bishop returned to the kitchen he went heavily to the stove, got the saucepan, and filled his coffee cup. He sat down. "Beryl, you shouldn't have done a thing like that. It's tampering with sacred things."

"I know it was wrong. I don't know why I did it. I was only trying to protect Katie. I won't have it! A lazy, no-good trash like Jack Whitetop!"

"But if his grandfather appeared to him—"

"His grandfather my foot! He got old Milo Ferguson in cahoots with him to make the story good. Imagine a real honest-to-goodness spirit appearing to an apostate like that! The whole thing's just as phony as the voice *you* heard. I wouldn't put it past either of them."

The bishop finished his coffee. He was feeling better. "I'm glad you told me this."

"I guess I didn't think."

"It was the wrong thing to do, but you were a mother protecting her child. It certainly takes a load off my chest. I should have realized. I'm not worthy of a heavenly message. I'm not the type. Some people have them and some don't. If it was going to come to me it would have been before now."

"If you don't think you're worthy, what about that trashy Jack Whitetop? Not to mention that apostate and his vile cigars."

"A sheer imposition," the bishop agreed, judging the whole from the part. "That scalawag! He's obviously in cahoots with Milo. The pair of them trapped poor Henry into marrying Anita. And Jackson never so much as opened his head before Milo brought that Toolson woman. I remember now, he'd say he wasn't going to marry Anita. But never a hint that Milo would show up. Served him right if Milo had been a little late."

"I think Henry *should* marry Anita," Sister Jensen said. "After all. And I'm thankful for Katie. What if that beast had married her and the mess had come out later?"

"We've got Jackson to thank for that much."

"Now, don't you go thanking that trash."

"Give the devil his due. But I must say," the bishop mused, "that for a cheat and a liar he's showing remarkable brass. You can't shake his confidence."

"Don't go talking that way. Show a little confidence of your own the other way."

"Beryl, we need a rest. Do you know that we've never really had a vacation since we've been married? And Katie's upset, poor child. She needs to get away from everything for a while. Why don't we take a trip?"

"Do you think we can leave things?"

"The place can get along without us. When can you be ready?"

"We haven't unpacked from this morning."

"We'll leave after supper," the bishop decided. "We'll stop in Salt Lake for Conference, and then—Beryl, we've never made that trip we've always planned on, back to the old country."

"Oh, Waldo!"

"I'll get Ned Holt to take care of the place. They say he had a falling out with Henry, and he'll be wanting something to do. We'll leave after supper."

CHAPTER
TWENTY-NINE

It had been a hard day. Jackson made supper over an open fire in the yard. The old stove had simply fallen to pieces on being moved out of the house. Or perhaps, like the bed, the table, the sink, and everything else, it had been ripped apart in the search for treasure. The skillet had a brown crust burned onto it; he recalled he'd been browning Ned Holt's concoction in it at the time the two strangers arrived, and had left it on the stove. He scraped it clean and opened a can of beans into it. Everything in the house had simply been thrown out, and he couldn't find the coffee. The coffee pot, sitting among a pile of cans, was half full and he warmed it up. Luckily it contained real coffee, and he smiled, thinking the men remodeling his house were somewhat less than perfect Saints—but who is?

It was dark when he finished eating. Headlights of a car moved down the valley; he had no idea it was the bishop taking Katie out of his life. He scoured his skillet with sand in the creek, then saddled a horse and rode to the bishop's to do a little courting. He learned the bad news from Ned Holt, and came back. Now, that was a crazy thing for the bishop to do, he figured. Bishop ought to know there wasn't any possible way to prevent what had to happen.

There were a few live coals in the ashes of his fire. He put on bark and chips, fanned a flame, and then got some chunks from the woodpile. He turned to the fire and saw Henry Brown standing by it, a shotgun under his arm.

"Well, Henry."

"Put some wood on the fire." Henry's voice was a curious monotone, tight and squeezed dry by some emotion.

Jackson put three chunks on the fire. "How'd you get here? Walk?"

"Got a little business with you."

"Sure. I'd better put up my horse."

"You're going to use your horse."

"What's on your mind, Henry?"

Henry raised the shotgun slightly. "You come along with me to get my horse. It's back in the willows."

"O.K."

"And hop when I tell you!" Henry's voice was suddenly sharp.

"Just tell me. I ain't arguing."

They walked back to the willows. Henry swung on his horse.

"Now we'll go back and get yours."

They went back. Jackson swung into the saddle. "Where to?"

"You're going to take another look at the Jonah."

"I think you're crazy."

"Don't argue with me, Jack. I'm not in the mood tonight."

"There ain't no future in it, Henry."

"I guess you're right. Get going. A man can take just so much and then it don't matter."

"Look, Henry, it won't work out."

"Don't argue with me tonight! Get going! Nobody'll ever find you in an old shaft. People will think you chased off after Katie. Get moving."

"You're certainly riled up."

"Get going! I didn't come here to palaver."

Jackson swung a knee over the saddlehorn. "I'd be a damned fool to take a long ride like that just to get shot."

Henry raised the gun. "You think I'm fooling?"

"Hell, no. I never seen a guy in my life in deader earnest. But look at my side. If you're going to shoot me anyhow, I'll be damned if I'll make it easy for you. Go ahead and shoot."

Henry gripped the shotgun until his fists trembled. "I don't know why I ain't done this before."

"Well, you ain't had cause, very long," Jackson pointed out helpfully. "They'll catch you, Henry. You're being a fool."

"Nobody has to know who did it."

"I don't think you've thought this thing through. Sure, leave me up in the old shaft of the Jonah and it might of worked. But I won't go. Shotgun makes one hell of a mess, Henry. Shoot me and you might as well shoot my horse too, or he'll take off and drag my body hell knows where. Folks find blood and gore around here, and first thing you know they smell murder. And what about Milo?"

The gun wavered, "Milo?"

"He knows more about your business than you do. What about Ned Holt? He knows about it, too. And he's reformed. How long do you think it'd take the law to put two and two together? Kill me, you got to get rid of Milo and Ned Holt. That's the worst about this murder racket. No end to it. Don't you ever read murder books?"

Henry lowered the gun. "Oh, God." He'd brooded over the thing, and all his venom had centered on Jackson. Get rid of Jackson and he got rid of all his troubles. It had seemed so simple to take him to the abandoned mine.

"You're upset, Henry," Jackson soothed. He got off and put the coffee pot on the fire. "Why don't we talk it over?"

Henry put the shotgun in his saddle boot and swung off. "I guess I sort of lost my head. No hard feelings?"

"Forget it, Henry. Maybe I'll figure on murdering you sometime." Jackson was more relieved than he cared to show. "We all have our bad days."

Henry sat down in the dust and put his head in his hands. "Jack, I'm ruined. And, damn it, it's all your fault."

"Don't blame me if your chickens are coming home to roost. Would sooner or later anyhow. That's the worst thing about shady deals. You only got to miss once and you're finished up. Got to be too smart. A dumb guy can make mistakes all his life and maybe be right just once and own an oil well or something."

"Damn it, don't preach to me!"

"I'm not preaching."

"Jack, I'm done for. I've lost everything in the world."

"A fine way to talk on your wedding night. Let me tell you that you could do a lot worse than get Anita Smith.

O.K., you're disgraced. What does that mean? People still got to buy stuff at the store to eat, and if you can meet the mail order prices they'll get their other stuff from you, disgraced or not. You got a good ranch, you got your sheep. Plenty of men would be happy with half of it. All you lost is your position in the Church, and I don't figure you wanted that except that Katie come with it. You lost her, but what can you expect? You ought to be damned thankful that Anita will have you. You could do worse."

"I guess you're right, Jack. Is the coffee hot?"

"It'll do." Jackson poured two cups.

"This is something like it," Henry said. "This tastes like the real thing. I'll make the best of things. Anita will wait until I get back from prison."

"Who's throwing you in prison?"

"Aren't you going to tell, you and Milo?"

"All I want is what's due me. You get them books unfixed. And then you better send off a quick letter to the Collector of Internal Revenue. They'll hit you with a penalty, but that's all if you tell 'em before they find it out."

"Jack, I feel a lot better. I'm glad I had this talk with you."

"Call around any time," Jackson said, "when you feel like murder."

"I don't think I really would of, Jack. I never killed nobody in my life."

Jackson cocked an ear, then turned from the fire. Two very tired men came into view, limping pitifully. It was the pair who'd taken him to the Jonah in the green sedan.

"Why hello, strangers," Jackson greeted. "You sure do like to walk."

"Oh, no! Not you!" the little man groaned.

"My feet are killing me," the big man said.

"Look!" the little man said, pointing to Henry. "Look at who's here!"

"We been talking about you, Henry," the big man said.

"Now, wait a minute, men," Henry said. He got up. The big man grabbed him. The little man made a flying tackle. Henry yelled.

Jackson jerked the little man off and booted him in the seat of the pants. The little man sprawled in the dust. Jackson brought the heel of his riding boot onto the big man's shoe. The big man screamed and let go of Henry.

"Just for that," Jackson told the two strangers, "you can keep right on walking."

Henry's hands were clutching his back. His face was white and covered with cold sweat. "Jack, for God's sake do me a favor. Get on your horse and go get Charlie Littleface, quick. My back's out again."

CHAPTER
THIRTY

By the next afternoon the remodeling crew had proved beyond a doubt that there was no treasure hidden in the old house. "A lesson to us, Jack," Young Merrill Littlewall said. "Just goes to show what greed can do."

Jackson felt a bit blue. The valley seemed empty without Katie. He'd wondered if her going was connected with his having tried to get something for nothing. "Merrill, I won't hold you to it. I knowed there was nothing here all along."

"Oh, no you don't!" Young Merrill said quickly. "It's a bargain and we'll go through with it."

"You shook hands on it," Sid Worth pointed out. "You can't back out of it."

"No, sir," Reed Carter said. "That was the agreement. We'd fix the place up for anything we found in it. And that goes!"

"I didn't want to cause a ruckus," Jackson protested. "Sure, if you want to. Sure fine of you fellers."

"Well, I'll tell you," Young Merrill said. "It's worth it to us, Jack. Just look at what's going on. Here we got men from the south and men from the north, a-working side by side on a project. First time that's happened in years."

"Really get to know one another," Reed Carter said. "All pulling together with our shoulder to the same wheel."

"We're bigger," Sid Worth said. "Bigger and broader. We'll take our lesson like a man."

Jackson went out to the stable for his horse, and he heard the men back at the house burst into a roar of laughter. He grinned happily. Certainly was fine of them to be able to laugh at themselves that way.

He rode down to the store, in hopes there would be a card or something from Katie. There wasn't. "Leave any forwarding address?" he asked Milo.

"Nope. Bishop he said to me just to hold all mail, he didn't want to be bothered."

"When's he coming back?"

"Said he didn't know. Wouldn't start thinking about that for a few months anyhow." Milo puffed furiously at his cigar. "It's a dirty, low-down trick, is what it is. Stuff like that made me apostatize. Now look at Waldo Jensen. Bishop and all. Leader. Represents the gospel hereabouts. Example to others. And what does he do? Picks up and goes, and takes Katie with him. Apostle Black's mighty low, I hear. You're supposed to settle the Trouble. You're supposed to marry Katie. And he runs out on you. What if Katie meets up with some young buck and marries him when she's away? Fine thing for him to do. What can you expect from a bishop? What's he a-trying to do, make a liar out of your grandfather's spirit? Fixed the books up, Jack."

"How do I stand?"

"Henry and me worked late last night fixing up the account. Figured you had about five hundred more head of sheep, and squaring off the books for what your dad owed, you got forty-five hundred coming in cash."

"Sounds about right. And this is his." Jackson tossed the packet of hundred-dollar gold certificates on the counter. "Just leave what I got coming on account, and I'll draw on it."

"Henry's fixing up your income tax for you. He had power of attorney—" Milo's voice died. He was staring out the front window. "Well, doggone me," he breathed.

The bishop's car had pulled in. The bishop climbed out a bit stiffly and came into the store. "Apostle Black came back with us," he said. "We're holding a meeting in the schoolhouse. Tell everybody to be there, Milo. Everybody who drops in. Seven-thirty sharp. And I'd like a tank of gas. Jack, will you take my car and go around? I'm all in. We want everybody. Apostle Black," the bishop added quietly, "is very feeble. He shouldn't have made the trip."

Jackson sat beside Katie in the front seat. She ignored him completely. Apostle Black, beside Sister Jensen in the rear, was like a wax dummy. There was not the slightest sign of color in the face or lips; the hair was a dull dead white. His eyes were closed, chin sunk on his chest. Despite the warmth of the afternoon he was swathed in a black overcoat, with a shawl over his shoulders, as protection from the chill breath of death.

The bishop drove carefully. The pouches were deep and purple under bloodshot eyes; he was tired. Katie gazed straight ahead at the unwinding road.

"Stop!" The word was an explosion. The bishop jammed on the brakes. The frail gray figure in the back had come alive in a remarkable way. The eyes were open, glowingly open, dark eyes that burned. The frail figure was erect with a sudden surge of vitality.

"What is it, Brother Black?" the bishop asked anxiously.

Sister Jensen made soothing sounds. "Don't tire yourself out, Brother Black. We're almost there, now. It's been a long trip, hasn't it? You shouldn't have come."

"I see it!" the apostle cried. "I see it rising from the valley. White and gleaming. A testimony of faith. A place of worship. Built for the ages." A bony figure pointed out the car window. "There it is! Can you see it? A lovely meeting-house for the valley. I see it! There it will be!"

"The Spirit of the Lord is with you, Brother Black," the bishop said. "My land starts right over beyond that little rise. I will be happy to donate it as a site."

"Right *there!*" Apostle Black said, pointing to the little rise. "Right where that little square of white fence is. I can see it. That's where the church will be built."

"Or a few hundred yards to the south," the bishop suggested.

"Bishop Jensen, can't you see where I'm pointing? You see that little square of white picket fence? Enclosing something, looks like a headstone."

"It is a headstone," the bishop said.

"Oh, my goodness," Sister Jensen breathed. "Brother Black, I'm sure you're awfully tired. Why don't we talk about it later?"

"Then you see the place," Apostle Black insisted. "On the little rise in that field. Where the white fence is. That is where the church will stand. I can see it now."

"Yes, Brother Black," the bishop said quietly. "So be it." And he drove on. The old man shrunk again, lifeless and motionless.

Katie turned wide eyes to Jackson, who shrugged. That particular square of meadowland was the only piece of property in the entire valley which could not possibly be used as a site for the church. It belonged to Milo Ferguson. The little white fence on the rise enclosed the grave of his wife Abbie. Nothing in the world could get title of it from the apostate.

The old man was asleep when they reached the bishop's place. Sister Jensen awakened him, and with Katie helped him into the house. The bishop regarded Jackson a long moment. "Brother Jackson, it's been a hard drive. Last night and then today. I'm tired. I just want to say—" He hesitated, forming words in his mind.

Ned Holt came out of the house. "Back earlier than I figured," Ned said, with considerable understatement.

The bishop nodded. "Change of plans. But we'd like you to stay on anyhow if you can. Could you give a hand on the luggage?. . . Notify everybody," he said to Jackson. "We'll meet at seven-thirty."

"Yes, sir. Brother Black sure looks feeble, don't he?"

"He's a dying man, Brother Jackson."

Jackson drove away wondering what had happened that the bishop again was calling him brother.

In his bedroom, the bishop said, "Beryl."

His wife was unpacking a suitcase. "Yes?"

"Do you feel the way I do? It seems that everything that's happened the past three days has had to happen. If we hadn't gone to Salt Lake—well, I don't know. He's awful feeble."

"You're tired. Why don't you lay down until suppertime? Katie and me'll fix something up right away."

"I've got to settle things in my own mind. The ways of the Lord are mysterious. What prompted you to speak into that milk can?"

"I've told you. I'm sorry about the whole thing. I told you a dozen times."

"But look at it this way—as long as I thought it was a voice from beyond, it had the same effect on me as if it *had* been. Then you told me about it. If you hadn't told me about it we wouldn't have been in Salt Lake this morning."

"It's merely a coincidence, Waldo. Don't go reading things into something that isn't there. I've heard you talk about that very same thing. You've criticized Sister Ormand for doing the exact same thing."

"I'm all mixed up, Beryl. But let's say for instance lightning kills a man's horse from under him and the man figures it's a miracle. Because he was spared he reforms and devotes his life to good. If it does that to him does it really matter whether or not it was sheer accident?"

"Lay down and get some rest, dear. Your eyes look awful. Poor Brother Black. He shouldn't of made this trip."

"He can't last long."

"Waldo, promise me something. Whatever happens, don't let it shake your faith."

"He was inspired. You could feel the spirit of the Lord as he pointed to the site."

"Waldo, promise you'll try. Don't base your faith on any one thing. The days of miracles are over."

CHAPTER
THIRTY-ONE

The big north room of the schoolhouse was crowded, each desk occupied by two people and the overflow standing along the sides and back. Everybody was on deck, Saint and sinner; this was something nobody wanted to miss. Milo, a bit defiant and a bit amused, seemed slightly undressed without his cigar. Henry and Anita were at a desk, their child asleep in a blanket on the desk top. Old Nephi Smith stood at the rear of the room, arms folded, eyebrows jutting, as he contemptuously surveyed the folks assembled for this foolishness. His jaws occasionally chomped, and a thin brown line of tobacco juice was faintly visible at his lip corners. Sid Worth, Young Merrill Littlewall, and Reed Carter were together at the rear. Ned Holt and Beulah Hess had one of the forward desks. The bishop and Apostle Black sat at the teacher's desk up front, facing the audience. The old man was snoring gently. Sister Jensen was on the stool at the battered organ; Katie was standing among the crowd in the rear, beside Jackson.

"I hope something comes of it," Katie murmured.

"It'll have to," Jackson said confidently.

"He's so old, the poor lamb. His doctor told him not to

make the trip. If anything's going to come of it, it's the last chance."

The bishop opened the meeting with prayer, and Sister Jensen played for a hymn. The bishop cleared his throat. "Brothers and sisters, you all know why we're gathered here this evening. I and my family we started on a long trip, just last night. But we're back. When we got to Salt Lake we heard that Apostle Black was—" he glanced around to make sure the old man was still snoring— "was very, very poorly. So this morning we called to pay our respects. He was feeble; he'd been bedridden for six weeks, and wasn't expected. . . But I wish you could have seen his face light up as we walked in. It was wonderful. And he said now he knew. Now he knew why he couldn't—" another glance around— "why he couldn't die. Nothing would do but that he should get out of bed and come back with us immediately. Strictly against doctors' orders. And as we drove along the valley this afternoon he pointed to the spot where the new meetinghouse will be built. It was Brother—er—it was Milo Ferguson's pasture."

A murmur ran through the crowd. Eyes turned to Milo, who glared back.

"Try and get it," Milo growled.

"Brother Black." The bishop shook the old man gently. Apostle Black came awake, blinked, oriented himself, and got up with the bishop's help, clutching the desk before him.

"I am old and I am tired," he announced, which was all too painfully obvious. "I have lived a long life and I'm ready to go on. But when I got ready to go I couldn't go, and this morning when Brother Jensen arrived I knew why

I had to stay. There was still something I had to do. And I am here this evening to do it. I've got the authority and I want to see the whole thing buttoned up tonight. As we drove through the valley I suddenly saw your new meeting-house appear on a field, all white and gleaming bright. I had the car stopped and I pointed out the spot. Tonight I will dedicate that spot, and take back with me your pledge of money and materials to build the meetinghouse. And then my work here on earth is finished."

He sat down with the bishop's help. The speech had been short and to the point. And it was impressive. There had been no chiding or carping about the past; there was nothing grand but indefinite in the rosy future. No ifs, ands, or buts. It would be done, Apostle Black said simply, tonight.

"I will start the ball rolling," the bishop said. "I pledge a thousand dollars. Who's next?"

There was a moment of silence when anything was possible. The thing was rolling. One man, rising to follow the bishop's lead, would start a parade.

Nephi Smith's voice cackled scornfully. "What good's your thousand, Bishop? Where you going to build the thing, on a balloon? You won't git that land off'n Milo!"

"I still got my voice," Milo shot across the room. "I can talk for myself."

"Well, don't git hostile. It's the truth ain't it? You buried your wife Abbie there, and no psalm-singing gospel shouters is going to disturb her bones. You and me, we're just here to see the fun. We ain't got no truck with this gospel racket."

"Whether it's true or whether it ain't don't cut no ice,"

Milo snapped. "All I said is I can talk for myself. You keep your big nose out of my affairs."

"Men, men," the bishop said. "We're not here to bicker. If you two want to quarrel, go on outside and do it."

"All right, kick me out," Nephi growled. "Shouldn't of come here in the first place." He began moving through the crowd, but his wife soothed him. "Got to spit anyhow," he protested, subsiding.

A titter ran over the room. "Try and kick me out," Milo bristled. "This here schoolhouse ain't owned by no church. It's county property and I'm a citizen and a taxpayer."

People were grinning. The bishop was haggard and helpless. The keynote of the meeting, that the thing was ordained and inevitable, had been rudely shattered by the bickering of the two apostates. At the organ, Sister Jensen ducked her head to conceal tears. Katie whispered to Jackson: "Those two old fools! It was moving. I could feel it."

"Anyhow," Milo declared, "I got something to say. I'm an apostate and I'm glad of it. Glad I had the guts to bust away from all that foolishness. All I ever got out of being a good Saint was lose everything I had in the world except one little piece of ground to bury my wife, Abbie. You got miles of land in the valley, but no, you ain't satisfied. You got to take away the only thing I got left."

"Of course we will pay you for the land," the bishop said.

"No, by golly! You won't buy it and nobody else won't buy it! My wife Abbie's bones ain't for sale! She was a good woman," Milo said. "We was together a long time afore she went away and left me alone. We had our ups and downs. Everybody does. But I never knowed what it was going to be like without Abbie, until she was gone. She was a good woman. And I put her there to rest on that piece of ground where we'd always figured on having our house. She liked that spot, and I remember the day we was married she went out there and stood up on that little rise and looked around—"

"Yes, Milo," the bishop said. "We all sympathize with you deeply, I'm sure."

"Don't give me that soft soap, Bishop!" Milo cried. "I got the floor and I got something to say."

"Sit down, Bishop Jensen," Apostle Black said in a thin voice that carried through the room. "Let him have his say. I've known Milo Ferguson a long time. He's a good man even though he did take the wrong turning in the road."

"Thanks, Apostle. Some dang fools around here don't seem to remember that this here is the United States of America and a man can say what he damn well pleases!" Milo glared about. "I'm an apostate and I want it understood first and last. I'm pretty old myself, but if anybody figures I'll soften up just on account of maybe I'll die sometime, they can think again." He sighed. "But my wife Abbie, she was a good woman. Firm in the faith to the last. And I guess now I know why it was old Moroni Skinner appeared to me. I figured it was on account of I should help out young Jack Whitetop. Couldn't see no other reason. But Jack can take care of hisself. I done a lot of thinking. Moroni he told me my wife Abbie was unhappy over there. And now I guess it was on account of she knowed what was going to happen and she figured I'd be ornery about it. My wife Abbie she knows me pretty good, and I'm a ornery cuss. But if she's going to be unhappy about it, why it's her business. It's her bones. If she wants a church there where we figured on making our house, why, there ain't no better site in the valley. I guess Abbie knows that. I guess she figures a church is the best building that could go on that spot she picked out. Me, I don't give a hoot if she wants it that way. If she wants to be there under the floor and be pestered by a bunch of hymns and preaching from now to eternity, why that's her affair. Never could understand a woman, nohow. When I die I don't want nobody singing over my grave every Sunday. But if Abbie she wants it, it's all right by me. You can have the land."

Beaming, the bishop arose to proffer thanks for the crowd, but Apostle Black's thin hand touched his knee and stopped him. There was a period of deep silence.

"Ahem!" Henry Brown, prodded by Anita, was on his feet. "I don't ask no forgiveness from nobody for what I done, and I'm not trying to buy my way into heaven. All I can do from now on is try to do better and hope in time to make up for it. But meanwhile I got to square up. I done plenty of thinking of late. See things different now. You can figure it out in dollars and cents. If you don't live right it will catch up with you sometime and you got to pay off with a penalty. Guess I always did know that, but I figured I was too smart. Now I know I ain't. I can get ahead without it. And anyhow it's wonderful to figure on squaring up and not being afraid to look nobody in the eye.

"Anita and me, we talked it over. Today I wrote a letter to the income tax people. Hope I won't go to jail. I'll pay up what they want, together with the penalty, and what's left—"

"Henry, dear," Anita whispered, tugging at his sleeve.

Henry sighed deeply. "What I mean is, I got better than eight thousand dollars tucked away. Some of it should of gone to the government. Some of it would of been mine anyhow. Some of it I took from folks who wasn't as sharp as me. If it's all right by everybody, we'll use that money to build the church. And what the income tax people want out of me I'll pay as I go along. I built up once and I can do it again. I want to start off square, and I don't guess there's a better way to turn that money."

"I can't imagine a better use for the money," Apostle Black said. "Next?"

Ned Holt was on his feet to get rid of his twenty-eight hundred and sixty dollars.

"Well?" Katie whispered to Jackson.

"Come to think of it," Jackson spoke up, "I never paid a cent of tithing in my life, or my folks before me. Figure I might as well square it up at a whack. Got a little coming on my sheep, and figure it ought to cover it. I pledge forty-five hundred dollars."

"You didn't have to leave yourself penniless," Katie whispered reprovingly.

"I was going to say five hundred," Jackson confessed. "But the 'forty' just slipped out."

"Now, wait a minute," Nephi Smith cried. "I donated the land the other time for the meetinghouse, and except I wasn't done right by, we might all be there tonight and there wouldn't of been no flood. And Milo ain't getting ahead of me. If that old fool can give his pasture, then I got a thousand dollars ain't doing me no good. I can be as good an apostate as he can!"

"Thank you, Brother Nephi," Apostle Black said.

"I ain't no brother, you old fool!"

"Not so far from it."

There was a small commotion in the rear of the room. Sid Worth was shoving at Reed Carter. Reed Carter was shoving at Young Merrill Littlewall. Young Merrill was shoving at Sid Worth. In this deadlock, Sid Worth cannily changed objectives, and Young Merrill was shoved out of the crowd.

"All right, I'll talk for the three of us," Young Merrill said with a hangdog expression. "I reckon we're ashamed of ourselves. We figured it was only the right thing, but I guess it was a sharper's trick. Wasn't really hidden treasure." Young Merrill ran a hand through his iron-gray hair. He seemed fascinated by his shoes. "Well, Sid and Reed and me, we been fixing up Jackson's house on account of we figured we'd find money tucked away someplace. Well, there wasn't any. But Jack he'd left a skillet full of some coffee substitute on the stove that he'd been cooking up. Old Indian recipe with a little added, and you all know what that tastes like. And the stuff in the skillet was burned black. Well, we tried it anyhow. And I guess that's the secret, to cook it until it's burned black. Awful good stuff when it's made right. Can't tell it from coffee. So we figured, well, the agreement was we'd have what we found, and we'd found that. So we organized a little company between us and we figured to make it and peddle it among the Saints. Plenty of money in it if it's handled right."

"I can testify to that part of it," the bishop said. "I've tasted Brother Jackson's Coffee-Near. Wonderful. And none of the harmful effects of real coffee."

"If it's all right with Jack," Young Merrill said, still studying the toes of his shoes, "we'd like to cut him in on it. And we'd like to donate ten percent of the profits for church maintenance. Never seen a meetinghouse yet that couldn't use a little steady income."

Jackson looked across the desks at Ned Holt. Ned shook his head; he didn't want to be an Indian trader with his cleansing sacrifice.

"O.K. by me," Jackson said. He confided to Katie, "Anyhow, it probably tastes as bad as all the other substitutes, burned black or no."

"Just what do you mean?" she asked, but he was paying rapt attention to a Saint who'd jumped up to pledge fifty dollars. For a few minutes people were crowding themselves to pledge anything from five to a thousand dollars, from a month's work to teams and scrapers. Then Sister Ormand got the floor and went into a long story about how she'd been told the whole thing beforehand in a conversation with the Lord. The bishop diplomatically turned her tap off, and everybody went in a caravan to Milo's pasture and Apostle Black dedicated the site.

"I'm very tired," the old man said happily. The bishop took him home.

"Won't you come in, Jack?" Sister Jensen asked in a friendly way.

"Well, thanks," Jackson said, surprised.

"Getting pretty late," the bishop said.

"Nonsense. Come in a minute anyhow, Jack," Sister Jensen urged. "I've got some chocolate cake."

"Beryl," the bishop said flatly, "those young folks want to be alone together."

"Dad, what put that into your head?" Katie demanded.

Her mother patted her arm. "I understand, dear. You'll run Jack down to his place in the car, won't you? And Jack, you must call around often."

"All right," Katie said. "Let's go, Jack."

With Apostle Black tucked in, the bishop went to his bedroom. His wife was sitting on the edge of the bed crying.

"What's the matter? I thought everything was marvelous."

"Oh, Waldo, I'm such an unfaithful fool!"

"Unfaithful?"

"Now, don't you go picking at words again! I mean, I haven't had faith. Everything's turned out so wonderful. Just like it was supposed to. And all along I fought tooth and toenail against it. I even deceived you. I mean tricked you."

"But it was all part of it, Beryl."

"And that's why I'm so happy," she sobbed. "It was a mean, selfish thing for me to trick you—and yet that was all part of it. Waldo, something must have prompted me. I wouldn't do a thing like that ordinarily. Something must have made me do it."

"That's how I've felt."

"Waldo, I've had faith because you had it and because I

wanted to be a good wife. But now I've got it for myself. It's so wonderful!" she wailed tearfully.

"There's still one thing," the bishop pointed out. "Katie."

"She'll marry him. I know it. I realized tonight there was no use fighting against what has to happen. And he's changed, don't you think? His grandfather changed, after a visitation. Old Moroni Skinner was a fine man. Jack's got the blood."

"But," the bishop said, "Katie has a mind of her own."

CHAPTER THIRTY-TWO

What I want to give you," Katie said, as Jackson drove the bishop's car down the valley, "is a piece of my mind."

"I'll take you piece by piece," Jackson said.

"And don't be smart. I never in my born life saw such a smug, insufferable hypocrite as you've turned out to be. You used to be a pretty nice fellow."

"Hypocrite?"

"You got Dad drunk yesterday. Don't deny it."

"Nephi gave him the cider."

"You might have warned him. How does he know the taste of alcohol? That cider had a spike that would knock your hat off!"

"How do you know?"

"And this Coffee-Near business. I don't know what jalap Young Merrill and the others found in your house, but I know what you gave Dad. I know real coffee when I see it!"

"Then why didn't you tell him?"

"That's what I mean. You think you're so smart lately. If I'd told him you were giving him real coffee he never would have forgiven you. Not in a million years."

"I'm glad you care about that."

"Of course I cared. Simply because I was interested to see how your crazy idea would work out."

"Working out right on the button."

"Jack, that's why I can't stand you. Don't you ever have a moment's doubt about *anything?*"

"Can't argue about what's going to happen."

"And I suppose now I'm supposed to throw myself into your arms."

"Well, no." Jackson stopped the car and took her into his arms. "I'll go halfway. That's only right."

"Jack, let me go!" She didn't struggle very hard. "Jack, you ought to be ashamed of yourself, taking advantage of me."

"Don't you love me?"

"I wouldn't marry you if you were the last man on earth."

"Don't you love me?"

"You're so sure of yourself!"

"Don't you love me?"

"Is the needle stuck?"

"Don't you love me?"

Katie sighed, and quit struggling. "Jack, I hate myself all to pieces."

He found her lips very pleasant. "I think there's a future to this."

"I ought to have more spine. I'm a jellyfish. I can't live with myself. I think we'd better go on."

Jackson continued down the yellow road, greasewood and sage flashing past on either side of the headlights. "What's wrong, honey?"

Katie sighed. "Jack, I'm old enough to make up my own mind about a thing like this. I did, and now I have to change it. Remember I told you about the soldier who went away and never came back? The ten glorious days with the only man I ever loved?"

"It takes time. I'm not jealous of him."

"Well, that's news! Who the devil did you think I was talking about?"

"I was away. I never seen the guy."

"You simpleton—it was you."

"Huh?"

"Jack!" Katie grabbed the wheel and steered the car back into the road. "Watch where you're going, for heaven's sake!"

"But I don't get it. I did come back."

"I thought so, too. But you went horizontal again as soon as you took the uniform off. Jack, you were wonderful on furlough. You know you're a handsome brute, and you were part of something and doing something. And that man never came back. So I made up my mind. And now I've had to change it and that's what I can't stand. It's so damned inevitable. I knew I'd have to."

"You sure didn't act like it."

"I'm tired of being shoved around. You're born and you get a first tooth and learn to walk and begin talking and your parents praise you, but what have you done? It's all down in the book, and you're just following the groove with every other baby in the world. You get new teeth and the boys tease you. Then pretty soon their voices change and they're bashful. You go out on your first date and before you know it you're dreaming about love as if you had discovered it for the first time in history. And you're helpless. Glands. Haven't you ever wanted to live your own life?"

"Well, I tried to," Jackson admitted. "Me, I figured the whole rat race was silly. I figured just to relax and to hell with it. Get plenty of rest and read some books and let the world go right on rat-racing. But look what happened to me. Now I got to be an eager beaver the rest of my born life. A wife on my hands and maybe after a while—well, I'm just one of the rats from here on out."

He stopped at Henry's store. Henry was in his living room playing cards with Anita and Milo. "Guess I got a little generous, Henry," Jackson admitted. "Could you advance me five hundred dollars to get married on?"

Henry got the money from the store safe. "Just like your dad, Jack. Never happy unless you're in debt."

"I guess I'm a hustler from here on."

"I know it; just a little joke."

"Jack," Katie said as they were going on, "I never looked at it that way. I thought you were just lazy trash. Actually, you had the courage to rebel against the rat race."

"I sort of was in practice," Jackson admitted modestly. "And my dad before me. Wait a minute. You're not marrying me just on account of you're supposed to?"

"Supposed to? I threw myself at you until I blush to think of it."

"If you threw yourself you sure put English on that throw."

"What about your furlough? When you came back I decided I'd be sensible and do the right thing. And you stopped calling around, anyhow. But the other morning when you came out to the corral and told me we were going to get married—Jack, you don't know how handsome you were."

"And you was all fixed to marry Henry."

"Afterwards? Jack, I had a little pride. And I didn't want to be shoved into anything. If I married you I wanted to do it for myself and not because I couldn't help it."

This wasn't very clear, but Jackson figured he wouldn't worry about that as long as it turned out O.K.

"Jack, let's not talk about that. Let's talk about—well, tomorrow."

"How about tonight?"

"You're almost home. I've got to get back."

"Full tank of gas. We can be married in the morning in Tooele. You know some folks there you can stay with tonight."

"Dad would be furious."

"I've met his conditions. My sheep are worth what I owe on the mortgage. And the Trouble's settled."

"The bishop's daughter has to go through the Temple. You're only a deacon."

"Plenty of good couples get married first just ordinary and go through the Temple later. I guess the bishop's son-in-law wouldn't have much grief getting promoted to elder and getting his bishop's recommend."

"Well, it's—just something nobody would think the bishop's daughter would do."

"I thought you wanted to live your own life. Anyhow, what if the minute I'm an elder they send me on a mission for two or three years?"

"Jack!"

When he reached the turn to his place he just kept right on going.

"Jack," Katie said dreamily, "think of all that's happened these past three days. It's never going to be dull, with you around."

"I've used up all that Grandpa Skinner told me," Jackson said thankfully. "I know what you mean about being shoved around. From here on I'm dealing off the wrist. Them that can see into the future can have it."

CHAPTER
THIRTY-THREE

Old Moroni Skinner was moving. It was on a Saturday, and since heaven had always been on a five-day week, which was one reason it was heaven, the neighboring angels were helping load up the heavy stuff on a cloud moored to the front gate. Moroni was happy. His grandson had come through handsomely. Yes, sir, Jackson had shown the true Skinner blood. Though privately Moroni had to admit, now it was all over and Jackson was safely married to Katie and in his remodeled house and working hard, and the meetinghouse was going up—he had to admit that during those hectic three days as he'd watched the records hour by hour he'd had some misgivings.

With his worries over, Moroni's work had improved. He'd been promoted to Chief Checker of the Compiling Office of the Accounting Section of the Current History Division of the Records Department, which was why he was moving into better quarters, for progress and glory are eternal.

"But just as you finally brought the load of diamonds and we made the rock garden," his wife Lucy complained, carrying the gold teakettle out to the cloud, "and the roof is fixed, we got to move. It's always the way. I wish to heaven that heaven would settle down one of these aeons. Always on the go. A body can't hardly get to know the neighbors and you're moving on. This eternal progress gets tiresome at times."

"I been thinking," Moroni said slyly. "I guess I'd better turn the promotion down."

"Moroni, I declare you vex me at times. All the worry of moving—why don't they fix railings on those clouds; you always lose something—and you'll turn the job down? I thought you was going to snap out of it after you took that trip to earth."

"All right, I won't turn it down," Moroni said. He understood Lucy very well, which was another thing that made it heaven. He'd never been able to fathom a woman on earth.

"And besides that, what about Brother Ivers, who's promoted to your old job? Turn the job down! Brother Ivers has got his right to glory and progression as good as anybody else. Turn the job down! Moroni, you grab that atomic bread baker and get it out to that cloud in a hurry and let's hear no more out of you!"

"Yes, Lucy," Moroni said. As he went out, a heavily laden cloud came floating up the gold-paved street and stopped before Moroni's pearly gate. Two angels, a man and a woman, were waiting atop the heap of their belongings.

"Brother Skinner?" the man said. "I'm Ivers."

"We're just leaving, Brother Ivers. Won't be only a few minutes more."

"Hate to rush you, Brother, but you know how it is up here. The others was waiting to move into our old place."

"Don't know why they're always so crowded up here," Moroni said.

"These wars and famines and things. It's temporarily over-crowded."

"You ain't been here long, Brother. Never has been no different. Well, it's a nice little place you're getting. I fixed it up good while I was here."

"It's lovely," Sister Ivers said sweetly. Moroni went inside for another load, and Sister Ivers said, "But I certainly wouldn't be caught dead with that rock garden in my front yard! Diamonds are so common. Can't we get some nice creek boulders?"

"Pretty hard to find around here." Brother Ivers sighed. He knew it would be creek boulders. Sometimes he wished a man didn't understand so much in heaven. Back on earth he'd sometimes felt, if only briefly, that he ruled the house.

Moroni and Lucy got on their cloud and wafted to the new quarters. "Say, this is classy!" Moroni said.

"But I certainly wouldn't be caught dead with that kind of paint," Lucy said. "Moroni, you'll have to get busy right away and redo the whole place."

"Yes, dear," Moroni said. He'd seen from the records that very day that Jackson was moving the bathtub and a closet and making an arch out of a doorway in his newly remodeled house. Good practice for the hereafter, look at it one way. Look at it another, Moroni thought, and you wondered just where the eternal progression came in.

He went outside glumly and saw Apostle Black walking down the street. "Well, Brother Black! Ain't seen you since you got here."

"Looking well, Brother Moroni," the other said, shaking hands. "But as I remember you was older, much older."

"You was younger."

"Well, yes."

"How do you like it up here?"

"Can't kick. They put me in the Destiny Department. I'm in Immediate Impending Events Section. Interesting work. Not much of a job, yet, but I got a promise of advancement. No end to promotion up here, I hear."

Moroni chuckled. "Immediate Impending Events, huh? Well, I'll bet their records look like hen tracks during that three days when I settled the Trouble in the valley and straightened Jackson out. They sure slipped up on that!"

"Didn't cross out a line; I looked it up," Apostle Black said. "It all happened exactly the way it was supposed to, them three days."

"But what about my trip to earth and appearing to Jackson and Milo?"

"Just like it was supposed to. Personally, I don't know why they have to have a Current History Division at all. We always know in Destiny what'll happen. And it always does. Ought to get a transfer, Brother, to somewhere where your work amounts to something."

"Well," Moroni Skinner said, "I'll be doggoned!"

ABOUT THE AUTHOR

Samuel W. Taylor was born in 1907, one of the thirty-six children born to John W. Taylor, a polygamist and an apostle in The Church of Jesus Christ of Latter-day Saints. Sam grew up in Provo, Utah. He dropped out of Brigham Young University just two classes short of a degree and began pursuing his career as a writer. In World War II, he served in the Army Air Force Public Relations Office in London. Sam has penned countless stories, articles, and serial pieces for magazines such as *The Saturday Evening Post, Colliers, Esquire,* and *Liberty.* His books include several works on the Mormon culture, such as *Nightfall at Nauvoo* and *Family Kingdom.* He is perhaps best known for the 1961 hit *The Absent-minded Professor,* produced by Disney Studios. He is married to Gay Dimick and lives in Redwood City, California. He and Gay have one daughter, Sara.